The Dog Under The Bed 3

What Happened Next

DJ Cowdall

http://www.davidcowdall.com

https://twitter.com/djcowdall

https://www.facebook.com/DJCowdall

ISBN-13: 9781711815558

ASIN:

CONTENTS

Other Works By DJ Cowdall

Novels

Missing

The Dog Under The Bed 1

The Dog Under The Bed 2: Arthur On The Streets

Two Dogs In Africa

Hypnofear

I Was A Teenage Necromancer: Book 1

I Was A Teenage Necromancer: Book 2: Supernature

The Magic Christmas Tree

The Kids of Pirate Island

53%

Short Stories

Inferno

Kites

Sacrifice

A Breath of Magic

Available from all good booksellers

ACKNOWLEDGMENTS

Thank you to

Adam Luopa for proofreading.

https://luopa.com

--

Cover Art by

**Cover Art by Olivia
Pro Design**

CHAPTER ONE

"Arthur!" Stan said quietly. His words were almost a whisper, barely able to give life to them.

Finally, after so long, so many cold nights, so long alone, a poor little dog without anyone to love him found someone who knew his name, who even noticed he was there.

*

We all love dogs, don't we? Not everyone does, and not everyone gets the chance to find out just how amazing they can be. This story is about one particular dog, who had only ever known love and comfort, and how after all that ended had to find his way, in life on the streets. Arthur is a wily dog, crafty when he needs to be, but he wasn't always that way. Any dog that goes from a life of love to a life alone will change, but just how much they change, and whether they can find their way back, is something none of us ever know until we take them into our homes and show them who and what we are. Then all we have is hope.

Stan looked at Arthur, completely aware of who he was, but no longer quite so sure of what he was. Far from being thin and worn out by the streets, somehow he had become unusually fat, big body, big bottom, but he still retained that sparkle in his eyes, that little mirror of love and kindness that the best dogs have. It gave him hope.

"I can't believe this is the same dog. He looks so," Nancy said, unable to finish her sentence.

Stan looked at her, hands on his hips. "I was thinking that, somehow he's put on weight, but his face looks different."

"I wonder where he's been," Nancy said, looking back at Arthur as he sat looking at them all.

From the time he had spent on the streets, he knew how unpredictable life could be. One minute you were laid somewhere warm, or had found something enjoyable to eat, and the next you were out in the cold, in the rain, or starving. He would take nothing for granted.

"He's very smelly," Stan said.

"You see, Billy, even Dad thinks you stink," Abigail quickly suggested, as ever unable to stop herself.

"Hey," Billy snapped, but it didn't matter, nothing would now, because he had someone new to play with, a new brother, one with four legs. Truth be told, he was a pongy dog.

"I guess we had better run a bath for him," Nancy said, turning to leave for the bathroom. As much as she accepted Arthur was part of their lives, or had been with Stan's mother, she knew he had been on the streets a long time. Just what that had done to him and his temperament, only time would tell.

"At least he's had all his shots," Stan said confidently.

"Nice, so we won't catch anything off you will we, Billy?" Abigail sniped, but her barbs were no longer so useful, as her brother was lost in a new world of doggy fun to come.

"Can he still sleep under my bed?" Billy asked excitedly.

"Er, I don't think so. We will just have to see." At that comment both Billy and Abigail groaned. It was a ubiquitous statement, one that all parents seemed to make when the real answer was no but they didn't want to hear the cries and moaning.

"Please," Billy pleaded.

"We'll see," Nancy shouted from the bathroom. It was a losing battle, but being children, they wouldn't give up. They would wait for the right time, around five minutes hence, and ask again. If either parent actually dared to say no, then they would have to wait longer, perhaps ten minutes.

Stan looked at the small dog, unsure of his own feelings over him. He knew all too well who he was, and what he meant to his mother. What mattered most was the connection he represented to his own mother, and all of the emotions that it brought. There were memories, endless memories, and lots of tears. He wasn't so sure he could face up to it, but it was like one of those challenges in life where there was only one option. He accepted we don't all get the choices we want, and this was perhaps one of them.

All the while Arthur remained, sat like the good dog he was, how he had been trained to be. As much as life on the streets had taught him to be wary, as well as crafty, he had come to love his short time in the house, its warmth, the food, but most of all the love they all shared. His instincts kept telling him to run, but his tummy and his laziness told him to wait and see.

As much as he knew he loved Billy and felt something special about Abigail, he wasn't sure of Stan, who appeared to give off a kind of reluctance to commit emotionally. It wasn't something that he could immediately see, more something he could feel. Arthur focused entirely on Stan, aware that he was the alpha, if he could ever be called such a thing, but he was certainly in charge.

"We're not really," Stan began to say, before biting his lip. His next words were to be *certain that we will keep him*, but it was a bit like saying no instead of we'll see, and from experience he knew very well what the reaction would be. It would have to wait, such a decision, because even he wasn't sure.

"Not really what, Dad?" Abigail asked, looking at him.

Stan looked at her. She was less enamored than her younger brother, obviously, but still, she had that look in her eye, she had connected in a way that he hadn't seen for too long. She was at an age where her emotions were uncertain about anything, so to see her perhaps engage with Arthur was a boon.

"Cat got your tongue?" Billy asked, bursting out laughing. He was sat close to Arthur, one arm around him, as if afraid that if he let go the lovely dog might run away suddenly.

"Dog got my tongue," Stan replied, smiling at them both. He turned his gaze towards Arthur, more to size him up as much as anything. The moment he did Arthur's ears dropped, as his tail began to wag. As he was sat his tail was partially trapped, so only the end of his tail wagged, ten to the dozen like a bird's wing. The rapping noise of it on the carpet caught Billy's attention, at which Abigail followed suit to look at him. To both of them he looked so cute, so shy and awkward, but at least Abigail would never say so; she was far too cool for that.

The moment Stan looked away, Arthur stopped wagging the end of his tail, his ears perking up. As soon as Stan looked back Arthur wagged again, as if he had a built in switch which activated only upon the boss's gaze.

Billy fell back, rolling around laughing, watching the little brown dog do his thing. He knew he had a friend for life.

"Right, gang, the bath is run, bring that mangy mutt in here," Nancy shouted, sounding happier than her words might have conveyed.

"Hey, that mutt has feelings," Billy shouted back, laughing ever harder if it were possible,

"She was talking about you," Abigail said, looking at her brother. She had a half mischievous smile, one that her brother knew well enough, so it made it alright. For now.

"Come on, Arthur," Stan said, turning slightly, all the while continuing to look at him. Arthur made to almost stand up, but he had been so long away from people who actually spoke to him, rather than at him, he wasn't sure if he was being called, or about to be thrown outside. He stood up, then back down again, then half stood, his ears fallen completely beside his head. Confusion reigned as he looked lost.

"Oh," Abigail said, feeling an unusual sense of emotion over anything other than a pop band.

"Come on, boy," Billy said, standing up quickly and slapping his leg. He had no idea what to expect, but to him he was no different than any other toy, such as a cuddly toy, but perhaps a far more cuddly and fun one. He did what felt natural.

"Bath time," Stan said, standing outside in the hallway. Arthur eventually settled on being stood up, but the moment he put one paw in front of himself, he decided they were going to evict him, back outside, where it was so cold he knew he wouldn't survive.

Arthur stood like a statue, not daring to move an inch in case the worst came true. He had run and jumped with children, and they had disappeared. He had walked lovingly up to people and they had shown him something very different in return. He felt a kind of fear he had become unaware of but which lurked inside of him each cold night outside.

They all stood and waited, as if frozen in time. Nobody knew what to do, except Stan, who felt he had to make the choice, so he did. Quickly he leaned in to Arthur as the small dog slunk back, wishing he could go and hide under the bed again. Before he could even think about running two large arms were wrapped around him, lifting him high up into the air. He had never been picked up in such a way before, as the old lady, the woman he loved so much, never had the strength to do so.

Arthur wriggled, his tail flapping around, as he wondered whether to cry or struggle and get free. He was a mixture of emotions, as on the one hand it felt good to be with someone, perhaps loving arms around him, but on the other he wasn't sure if they might choose to throw him out right then and there. It was all too much.

"Hold on now, Arthur," Stan said, trying his best to get a grip, but Arthur had put on pounds, and was much heavier than he ever remembered.

"Are you sure that really is your mum's dog?" Nancy asked. Stan froze on the spot, as even Arthur stopped wriggling. They looked at each other eye to eye.

Stan turned to look at her slowly, his eyes wide. He slowly turned back to look at the dog he was carrying, wondering deep down if perhaps he had made a huge mistake. The brown fur was thicker and much darker than he remembered, and of course he was a lot fatter, which was odd for a dog on the streets. It was hard to tell, but given the children around it was obvious he needed to be sure.

As the four stood, with Arthur in Stan's arms, all looking at him to see what might happen next, Arthur continued to look at the man holding him. His eyes were bright and wide open, a deep brown mix with a silver hint in the middle. Together they both looked at each other, for some sense of understanding and recognition.

"Dad," Billy asked, his voice hesitant, fearful of what he might do. He knew his father well enough that when he said something he would rarely change his mind. Even when he was wrong he wouldn't admit it easily.

Stan didn't respond to Billy, or look away, he looked a moment into Arthur's eyes. The small dog just waited, unusually patient for a dog being held up in such a way. Stan's expression changed, as if he saw something.

"It's Arthur, yes, it is Mum's dog," Stan said, his voice unusually quiet.

"Yes!" Billy shouted, at which Arthur jumped, once again trying to get free.

"Well that's good, time for his bath," Nancy said. She was well aware of the change in Stan's nature, but decided not to say anything. There would be time for a private moment later.

As Stan rounded into the bathroom, Arthur took one look at the toilet and immediately thought time for a drink, then he saw some bottles in the small sink and his heart skipped a beat. Then, finally he saw the bath, long and white and full of water, dreaded clean water. When he had been at home he never liked baths, so the kind lady would spray him with a hosepipe quickly, a smattering of soap and then he would run around in the grass out front. It wasn't perfect, but it was the best they could do together. The bath before him looked like a bottomless pit of water. Arthur scrambled all the more.

"I think he really wants to get into the bath," Nancy said, smiling. She was pleased to see he was so happy.

Stan had no choice but to put Arthur down, before he dropped him. Arthur took one look at the bath, before immediately turning in the opposite direction and running away as fast as he could.

Billy giggled loudly, before chasing after him, yelling at the top of his voice with excitement.

"What was that you were saying, Mum?" Abigail asked, standing beside her mother. "Seems he can't wait for a bath," she continued, the look on her face saying more than her sarcasm ever needed to.

"Don't you have a chicken to remove from under your bed?" Nancy said, quick as lightning. Her daughter's face dropped instantly, her mouth open as if to begin moaning.

"Nope, don't want to hear it," Nancy said, walking out as if she were in the process of dropping her microphone.

"Ha," Stan said, smiling at her as she walked away.

"Good luck catching the dog," Abigail said, walking out behind her mother. At that point the only one smiling was Billy, as he chased all over the house after the crazy dog.

"He's got to have a bath," Stan shouted, walking down the hall. He knew it, but wasn't sure how he might go about making it happen.

"Dad," Billy shouted, at which Stan quickly ran out and down the hall. He stopped at his son's bedroom, looking in to see Billy sat beside his bed, surrounded by toys.

"What's wrong?" Stan asked quickly.

Billy looked up at him. "Nothing, I was just wondering if I can put a saddle on Arthur and ride him?" he asked, his expression pure seriousness.

Stan looked at him, wondering how to answer, as Abigail suddenly burst out laughing. He thought how nice it was to hear her being so happy, even if it were over something silly.

"I don't think you can ride dogs," Stan said, not wanting to disappoint his son, but certain it was wrong anyway.

"Where is he?" Nancy asked, walking past.

"I'm here, Mum," Billy replied.

"No, I mean the dog," Nancy continued.

"He's here, under my bed," Billy said, looking back to the darkness underneath. Nancy and Stan both leaned over, peering in as a long dark nose poked out and two gleaming eyes looked at them. It was the oddity of Arthur, that look, so oblique, where it was impossible to tell whether he was happy or sad.

"I'll get him," Stan said, seeing his moment to shine, being the man of the house.

"No, love, leave him. I'll get him," Nancy said as she knelt down, lowering herself to look into the little dog's eyes.

All fell silent as Nancy leaned against her elbows, not blinking, looking into the twin beams of brown looking back at her.

"What's up, boy?" she asked, at which Arthur instinctively wagged his nervous tail.

"Maybe he needs some chicken?" Billy asked. Nancy wanted to laugh, but she wasn't sure if he was being serious or just gloating over his sister.

"Maybe," Nancy whispered. "What's up, boy?" she asked, her voice full of love.

"Well, I am hungry," Billy said, at which his mother turned to him and laughed lightly.

"Not you, silly," she said. "Arthur. I'm asking what he wants."

"Why, is he hungry?" Billy whispered back.

Nancy shrugged. "I'm not sure, we'll have to ask him."

Billy turned to look under the bed, staring intently at the silent dog. "Arthur, do you want something to eat?" he asked, at which Nancy laughed again. She sat up a little and wrapped her arms around her son. He followed suit, hugging her as tightly as he could. Arthur laid watching, thinking of the moments he had seen, the look on their faces, and how it felt, the warmth and energy they gave off. It was special, how it used to be for him. How he so much wanted it to be again.

Without saying anything Nancy lifted her hand out towards the dog, palm up. "Come on, boy. Want a hug?" she asked, looking and smiling at Arthur.

By then Abigail had stopped cleaning chicken away and came to see what was going on. It was unusually silent, especially in their house. No one was speaking as Stan waited by the doorway, looking in. All eyes were on Nancy and Arthur.

Slowly Arthur edged forward, his front paws grasping at the carpet. Billy moved slightly, thinking to hug him, but out of fear of frightening him again he waited.

"Come on, boy, come on, Arthur," Nancy said, sitting up straighter, holding both hands out, both palms upwards.

Arthur was cautious, but the moment she had shared, it seemed so full of love, so full of trust. He pulled himself free of the bed, slowly standing half up, until he was inches away from Nancy as she watched intently.

"Welcome to our home," Nancy said, as she delicately wrapped her arms around him. Arthur closed his eyes, allowing himself to sink into her. Together they stopped a moment, and shared a sense of love.

"Ohhh," Billy said quietly, wanting to do the same, but afraid if he did it might spoil the moment. Abigail thought to say something sarcastic, but couldn't think of anything that wasn't mean, so remained quiet. If Stan had thought to lift his arm and hug her, she would have welcomed it, a grateful reminder of when she was younger and never felt awkward about such things. It never happened, as Stan watched them, his mind a maelstrom of emotions, things that he felt but couldn't say. He wanted to express so much, but something deep down, a hidden emotion stopped him from doing so.

Finally Nancy looked up. "Right, let's try again, only a bit slower and give him time," she said, standing up slowly.

Everyone made way for Arthur, like a ceremonial procession. All except Stan, who was feeling very much the need to prove himself the man of the house, and the center of it. He quickly stepped past everyone, leaned over and swept his arms underneath Arthur. Nobody spoke or moved, unsure of what was going on. Arthur dropped his ears, ready to slink back and away. Whatever he could feel from Stan, it didn't seem particularly positive, more uncertain but bullish anyway.

"Right, up you go," Stan said proudly, as he shoved his hands under Arthur's body, taking a firm hold and lifting him into the air. Arthur was most definitely heavier than he looked, but there was no going back now. Stan gritted his teeth and heaved as best he could, as silently as he could, not wanting to give the game away.

Arthur wriggled for a moment, thinking to try to get free again, but it was obvious there was nowhere to go. His eyes were wide, as if he were experiencing a mixture of fear and uncertainty.

This was it, the moment, discovered, unwanted again and about to be thrown out into the streets. There would be snow, ice all over and nowhere to hide from it. The place he had escaped no longer existed, as a wrecking ball came crashing in. The pizza place might welcome him back, and the lovely lady, she never seemed to be around any more. So there it was, how it would be, how it always was, on the streets, back to his search for somewhere warm, looking for someone who might understand how to be kind to a lonely dog.

"I don't think he's enjoying that," Nancy said to Stan. She had stood up with him, folding her arms, sharing the expression of uncertainty that Arthur had.

Billy didn't say a word, wondering what was going to happen. He was prepared to scream and cry if they couldn't keep him, but he was old enough to know that with Dad, when you cried and complained, it didn't matter how much you did it or how loud; if he said no, it usually meant no.

Abigail shared their uncertainty, but determined to remain disinclined, if only in appearance. She tried to remain nonchalant, mildly disinterested, even though she too would be shocked to see the poor mutt kicked out. Still, she was at an age where she could handle anything, and look cool doing it.

Stan staggered, turning slowly as he lifted Arthur around. He nudged past the doorway, delicately avoiding accidentally crushing anyone on the way.

"Stan," Nancy said, her voice trailing off, but she feared for the worst.

The three watched as Stan walked out of the door, moving carefully along the narrow landing. Billy stood up, taking a hold of his mother's arm, as Abigail stood beside them both. They all watched, and waited, unable to find anything to say that would make a difference.

Suddenly Stan stopped. Without looking at them he quickly turned and entered the bathroom.

"Oh," Nancy said, as she quickly realized what was going on. She briefly nodded to both of her children, smiling, before following.

"Right," Stan said again, still holding Arthur in his arms as best he could. "Let's get this hound cleaned up," he continued, beginning to lower him towards the half-full bath.

Arthur could feel the heat from the bath water, as mild as it was. The scent from the water filtered through his flaring nostrils as he wondered if now was the time for panic. His flailed his legs, then waited to see if he would be released.

As Stan was struggling to contain him, Nancy, Billy and Abigail quickly entered the room, standing by the door, waiting to see what would happen. Billy looked up at his mother, feeling hugely relieved that their dog was going to be washed, and not evicted.

Stan began to give way, as Arthur struggled all the more. He glanced down, seeing the clear water, no soap, but still it was water, and flailed even more.

"Come on, boy, you need a good scrub," Stan muttered, as Billy began to laugh.

"I think," Nancy said.

"Yeah, " Stan said just as he dropped Arthur right into the bath. Water splashed all over, draining as much onto the floor and walls as it did onto the poor dog. Arthur flipped around, head under the water before quickly springing back out, leaping up as his paws refused to gain traction on the smooth surface.

"Bombs away," Abigail shouted, as Billy continued to laugh at it all.

"You're going to drop him," Nancy said, finishing her sentence. She was fully aware that it was after the fact, but it would provide more emphasis for what she knew even before it happened. They all did, except Stan. It was obvious he was a good husband, and a good father, but he had lots to learn about dogs.

"Oh, right, well," Stan said, standing up to look at the family. That was Arthur's cue, ready to make a move of his own. Instead of trying to claw at the tiles or smooth bath, he simply leaped further up, using his hind legs to push himself free, up and over.

"Wait, stop," Stan shouted.

"Get him," Nancy shouted.

"Run boy, run," Billy shouted.

Arthur sprang from the bath, skidded onto the smooth flooring and swept away, out of the room. He looked urgently one way, then the next, saw the stairs and away he went, as water splashed from him, dripping all over.

"Stan, he's ruining the carpet," Nancy called, looking at her husband as if he were like Billy, young and foolish.

"Go, Dad, go," Abigail shouted, wanting to laugh but not wanting the shatter the illusion of her being so in control, and uninterested.

Stan tried his best to follow as Arthur dropped quickly down the stairs and away. Water from his drenched coat soaked the walls and floor, but there would be no stopping him.

Stan ran down the stairs, shouting for the dog, calling his name.

"Quickly, Stan, do something," Nancy pleaded, following him.

"Give him some food," Abigail shouted, pleased with herself that she seemed to be the only one with a sensible thought about it.

"Yeah, Dad, get him some chicken. Abi has some under her bed!" Billy shouted, laughing so much he wanted to fall over.

Finally Arthur was cornered, back down the stairs at the bottom. He was in the hallway, on the cold floor, all doors closed, eyeing the frosted window of the back door. If it were open, out he would go and away again. Just open the door, he would be off, no more fuss, no more shouting.

Stan stood at the bottom of the stairs, breathless, looking at the dog. Arthur looked at him, his ears down, tail between his legs, looking so wary. He glanced from the man, to the door, then to the man again. It was obvious what he wanted.

It was a thought, an easy way out, a simple solution. As easy as it might be, he could never do it, never do that to Mum's dog. Arthur was a part of her, and as difficult as it was to come to terms with her loss, he knew his responsibilities lay deeper than to just his emotions.

Then, an idea struck him. "Billy," Stan shouted.

Billy came charging down the stairs. It was as much a relief that he didn't fall as anything else. "Yes, Dad?"

"Billy, would you please quickly get me some of the cooked sausages from the fridge," Stan said, looking down at his son.

Billy smiled, running back up without saying a word.

"What," Nancy began to say, as Billy charged past so fast it seemed he might not be able to stop.

Billy ignored her, running into the kitchen, opening the fridge door and scanning for the sausages. There they were, a plate of them, all cooked, cold but tasty. He grabbed at the plate, ensuring none spilled and ran back out, struggling to be hasty while holding them steady.

"Billy, the door, close," Nancy tried to say, but before she could finish her sentence he was gone.

"Here you are, Dad," Billy shouted, running so quickly down the stairs he seemed like a blur. Just as he saw his dad, standing in the hall, off he went, tripping as he was wont to do, sending the plate of sausages flying as he rolled over and over.

Stan looked around just in time to see his son flying through the air, still holding barely onto the plate, as sausages flew away, past him onto the hall floor. Almost as if deliberate, the sausages rolled across the floor, spreading out, resting neatly in front of their new dog.

Arthur stood up, his tail wagging intensely. He looked at Stan, then the young boy as he lay in a heap at the bottom of the stairs. Arthur had a look about him, that he couldn't quite believe his luck, or understand what on earth was going on. One minute they were dropping him into water, then the next they were shouting at him, and next thing they're throwing meat at him. He was both excited and afraid all at the same time.

"Well I was going to tempt him with a sausage, but I guess he'll be eating them before I get the chance," Stan said. He was standing, hands on hips, looking at his son. All he needed to do was tap his foot and he would look like a cartoon character. Billy looked at him, wondering if he should say that, but decided against it given the circumstances.

"It's fine, Dad," Billy said, struggling to stand up faster than his body would allow. "We can still do it," he continued, running again to grab at the sausages. The moment Arthur saw the boy run, his instincts kicked in, that look, that behavior, it only meant one thing: play!

Arthur leaped at the sausages, trying to grab one to gobble it up, as Billy did the same. It was a battle, where only the strongest would survive, and get a sausage. Billy grabbed at them quickly, giggling so much his sides hurt. Each time he tried to get another, Arthur naturally grabbed at the same one, as if it were a pop up game where they needed a mallet to hit the mole before it disappeared. The two seemed to show a unique connection, where each understood the other. Arthur had a mouth full of teeth, but not once did he show any signs of being a danger or a nuisance, instead he was as much involved in the game as the young boy.

Stan watched, smiling as he did. He wasn't even aware that he was smiling, or how he felt, simply being there in the moment, understanding that the two mattered to each other, and that a bond had been created. Stan had little understanding of just how much Arthur had been watching Billy play, or how much he had come to be a part of the house and its family. If he had known, he may not have felt so uncertain of his own feelings.

"Did you manage to save any?" Stan asked.

"Yeah, I got one," Billy said, giggling so much he struggled to speak. The moment he spoke, Arthur jumped at him, grabbed at the sausage in his hands and gobbled it all up. He was so excited, so full of food, he began to drool, his tail wagging so much his body shook. It was the last straw, as Billy could no longer cope with how funny it was. He broke down laughing even harder, so much that it became infectious, as Stan laughed a little, before feeling an unusual sensation, the urge to giggle with him.

Arthur began to lick at Billy's face, sniffing around him, nudging him. It was just too much, as Stan burst out laughing, joining his son in the fun.

"What's going on?" a voice called from behind. Stan turned quickly to see Nancy behind him, looking more concerned than he had expected.

"Oh no, don't let him lick you, you don't know where he's been," Nancy called, her face a picture of concern.

"Yes, Arthur, you don't know where Billy's been," Stan said, shocking himself that he had a sense of humor he knew nothing about.

As Nancy was about to chide Stan for his silliness she too was interrupted by giggling, only from behind her, as Abigail stood watching them all.

They all turned to look at Billy, as he had settled, sitting with Arthur, as the dog laid across him, panting away. They both looked happy, as if they had never been apart. It was a good thing, for Stan at least, but left more questions for himself than anything else.

CHAPTER TWO

Arthur was looking unusually tranquil, at least unusually so for a dog that was sat in a bath of water. The family were stood in the doorway watching, as Stan sat on the closed toilet nearby, watching too. Arthur had a serene look on his face, which seemed quite at odds with him being sat with water up to his shoulders.

"He seems happy enough," Abigail said, at which Arthur looked at her. He was still panting a little, his ears up, eyes wide open, suggesting he was content enough.

"Well, should we do something?" Nancy asked, wondering why Stan was just sitting looking at him.

"I think so, I guess we should wash him or something," Stan replied, wanting to do something but not really enjoying the idea of doing it.

"Can I get in with him?" Billy asked, excited as ever.

"No, of course not," Nancy said, horrified by the idea.

"Foolish boy," Abigail whispered, back to her usual self.

"Oi," Billy said, looking sharply at his sister.

"Of course you can't get in the bath," Abigail began.

"Cos I might give him fleas," Billy interrupted, well aware of what she was like by now. Abigail laughed, wanting to say more, but as sarcastic as she needed to be, she found her brother's self-awareness quite charming.

As Stan stood up to find some suitable soap, a lapping sound stopped him in his tracks. As he looked around he saw Arthur drinking the water that surrounded him.

"I wonder if he thinks it's a huge drinking bowl?" Nancy asked. She didn't laugh, but continued to look at the dog as if she were deeply curious by his manner, in some kind of scientific appreciation of his actions.

Stan looked at her, quite bewildered that she might honestly be serious about it.

Arthur continued to lap at the water, annoyed that it was so warm, but it was tasty anyway. He stopped mid lap, looking around to see them all staring at him. His mouth hung open, tongue half out, eyes peering around, wondering if they were going to do something. He was all too aware that with the family, anything was possible.

"Mum," Abigail asked.

"Yes, love," Nancy replied.

"Why is he doing that?"

"What, love?"

"That, his mouth open like that. Is he drinking, or letting water fill his stomach, or what?"

Nancy shook her head. "Not a clue, love."

Stan picked up a bottle of baby shampoo, leftovers from a long time ago, used to protect Billy's eyes. He leaned over, as Arthur closed his mouth and watched every move he made.

"Right, this will be nice, and when I'm done, you will smell lovely, and then it will be time for hugs," Stan said, hovering and waiting, as if he were wary of something.

"I don't want a hug," Abigail said.

"Who gets a hug?" Billy asked.

"Your dad is going to hug the dog," Nancy said, giggling quietly to herself. Stan looked at her with a mixture of fright and surprise.

The shampoo poured onto Arthur's neck and oozed down, as Stan spread it down his back.

"Can I have a go?" Billy asked.

"Not yet, son, let me clean him first," Stan replied, wanting nothing more than to up and go and leave anyone else to do it. Of course, responsibilities and all, he had no choice but to carry on and he knew it.

To Arthur it wasn't too bad. He had been given baths before, although less water and in a bowl instead of a bath. As annoying as it seemed, the water was warm and welcome, and he could remember just how good it would feel after. He had big plans for *after*.

"I have to go, got something to do," Abigail said, turning to walk away.

"You're not helping with our new dog?" Nancy asked, looking at her. There was more to it than a simple question, it was much more loaded than that, but it didn't actually have to be said, simply implied.

"Yeah, I have something to do," Abigail replied.

"Oh, what's that then?" Nancy asked.

"Anything but this," Abigail, determining to ignore anything else that was said as she walked away. She could feel her mother's gaze focusing on her, but no matter what she wouldn't look back.

"Don't forget your chores," Nancy said, as she stood arms folded in the bathroom doorway, watching her daughter go.

Stan scrubbed away, noticing how the water quickly changed from clear to a muddy brown. "Wow, he is dirty," he said.

"Just like Billy on bath night," Nancy said as she patted her son lovingly.

Billy slowly turned to look up at her. "You do know I'm not the dog here, don't you?" he said, sharp as a tack.

Nancy looked down, unsure whether to laugh, or what to think. He may well have been young, but he didn't miss a trick.

"Right, be thankful that you and Arthur get to have a wash in the bath, and not a hosepipe outside."

All the while Arthur remained sat, relaxed and happy that even if he was stuck in a large amount of water, at least it was warm. He knew how cold it was outside, as the steamed up windows were betrayed by incessant snow and cold.

"There, that seems good," Stan said, just at the point where Arthur was covered in a thick coat of white foam.

"He looks like a snowman," Billy said, smiling at Arthur.

"Yeah, he can go outside and play in it, if he likes," Stan said.

"Yeah, and then back under my bed," Billy replied, as happy as could be.

"Oh, well, we'll see," Stan said.

"Where were you thinking of him staying?" Nancy asked, feeling curious.

"Well, the shed might be a good idea," Stan replied, feeling confident in his choice.

"What?" Billy shouted.

"Pardon?" Nancy asked, sounding stern.

"Seriously?" Abigail called, surprising herself at being shocked enough to want to comment at all.

"Well, erm, I was," Stan spluttered, realizing he had nowhere to go.

"Mum," Billy said, tugging at his mum's top. He looked at her with his own set of puppy dog eyes. He didn't need to say any more, the tears threatening to flow were enough.

"Don't you worry, Billy, your dad will be the one sleeping in the shed."

"No, no, he can sleep in here, we will have to get some kind of bed set up," Stan said quickly, backtracking before anyone could say anything.

"Yay," Billy said, job done, battle won.

Stan didn't wait for anyone else to speak, instead taking an empty plastic jug from the side. Filling it with water he slowly poured it over Arthur's coat, wiping away the soap and foam.

"I think he likes that," Billy said, enjoying the spectacle.

"Yeah, I think he does. He seems such a good dog," Nancy said, feeling pleased with the new addition to their household.

"Yeah, he is, I mean that's what," Stan began to say, at which Arthur took his leave, leaping properly from the bath out onto the tiled floor.

Water followed him, cascading like a fountain of mud, fluff and dog all over.

The moment Arthur landed on the floor he became instantly aware of just how slippery it all was, as his paws slid and moved about with the water.

"Arthur!" Stan shouted, trying in vain to take hold of him.

"Get him," Nancy shouted, instinctively flapping her arms around, as if she might coax him into stopping whatever he was going to do.

"Here boy," Billy shouted, leaning over to try to gain his attention.

"Run boy!" Abigail shouted, as always wanting to be different.

Arthur had managed to find his feet, stood between the sink and bath, just long enough to see the commotion around him. He had thought it wise to stop and wait for instructions and for everyone to calm down, but the moment he heard the magic word, that sound which always told him how to react, then he had no choice.

"*Run*," Abigail had shouted. So he did. At first his paws slipped again, like an antelope on ice. He flapped some more, tried to run, then went for it.

"Come on, boy, come to me," Billy said, arms out waiting for the hero's welcome. Arthur sprang at him, crashing past, knocking him flying. Billy fell back, immediately coated in brown fur, drenched.

"No," Nancy shouted, as if that one word might somehow calm everything down.

Stan simply looked on, accepting his limitations, deep down knowing he would be dealing with the aftermath and not preventing a thing.

Arthur managed to escape into the hall, before standing a moment to look around. Water dripped from his coat, as he thought to shake, but knew he had to get somewhere, anywhere, because it was time to *run*.

"Arthur," Abigail shouted, laughing at the fun. For her the fun was the mess he was making as water flew around onto the walls and floor as he moved.

That was it, that was all he needed, the only motivation to go for it, so he did, running quickly towards her. Abigail's eyes lit up as she realized what the dog intended as he bounded towards her. She was sat on her bed, door open, enjoying the crazy moments, but she hadn't reckoned on how crazy it would be.

"No, Arthur," Abigail screamed, as Arthur leaped towards her, jumping as high as he could, up onto her bed, bundling into her. Just as Billy came running out from the bathroom, his mother and father in tow, Arthur chose that moment to finally sort out his coat. He tensed, then shook, sending a fine but relentless slough of water across everywhere, including Abigail.

"Noooooo," Abigail shouted again, holding her hands over her face as if it might save her.

Billy laughed so loud his throat hurt. "Yeah, go on, boy," he called out, enjoying it so much.

"Arthur," Nancy shouted, her worst mistake, as Arthur quickly turned to look at her. It was another sign to run again. As he leaped off Abigail's bed, running down the hall Nancy was stood holding her hands out, as if welcoming him. She hoped to catch him, but to him it was an invitation to go even more mad. The family watched as Arthur shot past, head down, tongue lolling from side to side as he headed for the stairs like a runaway train.

"Do something, Stan," Nancy shouted.

"Mum, look," Abigail cried, standing in her doorway dripping.

Stan knew what he had to do, but he was no fan of running. Still holding the bottle of shampoo he quickly darted out along the hall to the top of the stairs.

"Go on, Dad, run," Billy shouted, his sides aching from all the laughter. He had never seen anything like it.

Stan grabbed a large towel, quickly wrapping it around his hand, ready to grab the crazy dog one way or another. As he got to the top of the stairs, there he was, Arthur, the runaway dog, going like mad.

"Right, boy, come on now," Stan said, leaning over to take a hold. All he saw was Arthur's wide open mouth and flapping tongue as he ran past him, back along the hall into Abigail's room.

"No," Abigail shouted, as she felt like crying. So much for all the fun. Arthur bounded onto her bed, immediately sitting beside her. She just looked at him forlornly, resigned to her fate.

"Stay!" Stan shouted, hunched over, pointing a finger at Arthur. For all the fun, it was hard work, so he remained sat beside the miserable girl, panting away, drooling onto the bed. It had been a good day so far, he felt fresh and clean, and had enjoyed a good run. For Arthur, there was only one thing missing.

Billy ran up to him, aware that he was finished his madcap moment. Stan followed close behind, having grabbed an old towel, he quickly draped it across the waiting pooch, wrapping it around him. Arthur remained where he was, quietly accepting what might happen next. Before, with her, the lovely lady, they would go in, and sit beside a lovely warm fire. She would sit and read, perhaps do some knitting, while he laid at her feet, warm, comfortable and settled. Now, anything could happen, because lately, anything did happen.

Abigail got off her bed without saying a word. She glanced back at Arthur as she walked out, a look of thunder on her face. Arthur's ears pricked up, his eyes glistening, as if deep within he held a kind of understanding that mirrored hers, where words were unimportant. Whatever she might have been tempted to say she held onto, aware that there was more to the dog that she had understood. She would wait and see.

"Oh dear, love," Nancy said, hands out towards her daughter, feeling sympathy for her predicament, but having no clue what to do about it.

"Abi," Billy shouted. At first she didn't want to look back, but as she reached the bathroom door she found herself unable to resist a look back.

"What?" Abigail asked.

"If you want a bath, you can. Arthur's finished in there now," he said, barely able to finish his sentence before he broke down laughing again. His sides ached, he had laughed so much. It was infectious, as Arthur turned to look at him, wondering what was so good.

Abigail glared, but before she could offer any kind of retort Billy called again.

"Abigail," Billy said, without waiting for a response. "If you need some shampoo, Dad's got it in his hand," he called, laughing even louder if it were possible.

Suddenly Nancy burst out laughing. It had been totally unexpected to her, having thought it mildly amusing, but her son's laughter and his crazy reaction with the madcap dog, it was all too much. A short burst of laughter broke out into a hoot, as she laughed in time with Billy.

Stan scratched his head, trying his best not to join in. He knew it was best to avoid an angry daughter at the best of times, but try as he might even he wanted to laugh about it.

"Yes, go on, laugh," Abigail shouted, turning to walk into the bathroom.

"Oh, love," Nancy said, briefly controlling herself. She knew it was wrong to laugh, but couldn't resist. Stan remained resolute, he would refrain from joining in.

"Will you be running around up and down the stairs to get dried after, sis?" Billy suddenly shouted. It was too much, as Stan burst out laughing too.

"Ooh," Abigail shouted, forcing herself to be angry.

"Now please, that's enough," Nancy insisted, feeling a terrible urge to continue laughing. "We don't want to all end up in the dog house," Nancy finished, once again laughing with them. It was fun, so enjoyable.

Unexpectedly, Abigail giggled, forcing her hand over her mouth. No, she couldn't laugh, it was serious, she was angry and needed to express it.

Nancy pushed the bathroom door, to see her daughter stood by the hair filled bath, hand over mouth, giggling away to herself.

All the while Arthur remained sat, his tail wagging. It had been an amazing day so far, one he hoped would end up even better. It just needed one more thing to make it truly wonderful: food!

CHAPTER THREE

"Right, hold on," Stan said, as Arthur sat on the floor in front of him. Having finally coaxed him down the stairs, he waited patiently in the hallway, hoping someone would realize what he really needed.

Stan knelt down, wrapping the old towel around Arthur's shoulders, rubbing him gently as he did. It was new to Arthur, as he had only ever known drying by a lovely fire, or more recently curling up somewhere cold while alone. No one had ever put a towel around him when he was wet, nor rubbed him in quite that way. It felt as if his ears might fall off such was the frenzy of it. Still, it felt good, as his fur fluffed up and his body shook. Arthur turned as best he could to look at Stan, eyes wide open, ear flapping about, chops jiggling this way and that. He looked directly at Stan, staring at him, feeling so good about himself in a way he hadn't for far too long.

Stan looked down as he dried the little dog, seeing something in his eyes, aware he was being watched. He knew whose dog it was, who he had belonged to, what it meant. It bought back memories, made him think.

"Dad," Billy said.

Stan abruptly turned to see his son kneeling beside him, looking at him as if worried.

"Yeah, what's up, Billy?" Stan asked.

"You were just rubbing him dry, and then stopped, staring at him. What's up?" Billy asked.

Stan looked at him, feeling surprised. "Sorry, son, I was miles away," Stan replied, quickly rubbing Arthur again, all around.

"Right, he's dried. I guess he needs to go into the back garden, to do his business," Stan continued.

"He might be hungry, want some food," Billy said, at which Arthur perked right up. It was like a commandment, an order to instantly stand to attention. There were two things he loved most in the world, sleep and food, though now he might find more to love with the people around him.

"Sounds like sensible thinking," Stan said, berating himself mentally for not thinking of it himself.

"You go get him outside, and I will see what there is for him to eat," Stan said, quickly standing up. The things he had been thinking of diminished to the back of his mind, his son providing a welcome block to the things he tried not to think of.

"Dad," Billy called again.

Stan didn't answer, he simply made eye contact with him, brows raised, waiting for the response.

"Can I call him Scooby Doo?" Billy asked.

"Call who Scooby Doo?" Stan asked, wishing he hadn't asked.

Just as he spoke Abigail came down, completely changed, drying her hair with a towel.

"Hey look, Abi and Arthur both like to dry their hair with a towel," Billy commented, quick as a flash. Abigail stared at him.

"Now, now," Stan said.

"Dad, I think it's a good idea, a different name for the dog," Abigail began. Billy looked at her in surprise, wondering why she was agreeing with him.

"No, I don't," Stan started to say.

"In fact," Abigail interrupted before he could finish. "I think it's such a good idea, that we should change Arthur's name to Billy. That way, when you want to get both their attention, just shout Billy, and both will come running." Abigail didn't wait for the answer from either of them, but she was aware as she walked away of Arthur, sat looking at her, tail wagging, as if he knew something she didn't.

"Dad," Billy called, but Stan had decided to simply follow the sensible lead of his daughter, and pretend it had never happened.

Billy was alone, in much the way he often had been as he had grown up. Only now it was different, because there was a dog sitting beside him, looking so pleased with himself. In a way it was odd, because in that moment the excitement had given way to an appreciation that it was real, and that this new dog would actually stay with them. As odd as it was, it was still good, because there were so many possibilities to come. Billy could barely contain himself, over what to do next.

"Hey, boy," Billy said, looking directly at the dog sat before him. It occurred to him that he had never spoken to a dog before, because always his parents had stopped him from approaching others, in case they were dangerous, as if they were all dinosaurs that might eat him.

As Billy spoke, Arthur looked up at him, feeling decidedly unsure. He knew what he wanted, but had no idea who was actually in charge, or what might happen next. Often in his better life he had wagged his tail, stood up and turned around a few times, and then he would get a reaction. He could go outside to do his business in the garden, or he might get to go for a walk, or have a treat or even proper food. Now it was different, the rules were different. He was different.

"Food, boy?" Billy asked, leaning over with his hands open, leaning on his legs, looking to all the world like an old man.

There it was, that word again, the one thing that excited him the most. Arthur stood up, his tail wagging more than ever. That was his way to reply, other than to whine, but the old lady had grown tired of his cries, so of course he couldn't do that.

"OK, boy, let's go find you some food," Billy said, as excited as Arthur was. Immediately he turned and headed towards the kitchen. As he passed the living room he noticed Abigail sat on a small footstool, as always in front of a mirror, brushing her hair as if she were heading for an awards ceremony. Dad was sat in his usual chair, reading a magazine, but Mum was nowhere to be seen.

As he walked into the kitchen he had expected to see his mother, but the place was empty. "Dad, should I give Arthur something to eat?" Billy called.

"Yes, go ahead," Stan replied, his voice betraying his being lost in an article or something.

That was good, he knew he had to feed the dog. Now all he needed to do was find something for him. Billy opened the wall cupboards, peering in. It was full of tins, all sorts of things, but he didn't fancy having to try to open any of them, so closed the door.

"Want some crisps?" Billy tried to ask, but as he turned to look at Arthur he almost fell over, as Arthur was so hungry he was stood like a shadow, right behind him.

Billy opened the fridge, looking inside. "What shall we get, boy?" he asked, surveying the food landscape. Of course, there was no chicken, why would there be? There were plates of meat, small bowls with peeled boiled eggs, packs of cheese, salad, jars of sauces and pickles. Nothing quite seemed right.

"I don't know, boy, just not seeing anything you might like," Billy said, turning to Arthur.

Arthur's ears dropped, his eyes wide and sad. He had no idea what Billy was on about, but the boy was looking back at him, and had no food in his hand, so clearly it wasn't good news.

"Hold on," Billy said, very much in tune with what was going on. He reached in, took hold of a plate of sliced meat and took it out.

Arthur felt an immediate sense of excitement, as he wondered of the scraps he might get, or even an entire slice. It was a rare thing to be given such treats, but the boy seemed nice, and with him perhaps anything was possible.

Billy looked at Arthur, then to the fridge, wondering what their new dog might like. It was a tough choice, because he knew what he liked, but had no idea whether dogs were picky or not.

"Here you go, boy," Billy said, bending over to put the plate on the floor. He let it go and stood up, as Arthur stood likewise, looking so excited it appeared he might burst.

Arthur was hesitant, pacing around, his tail wagging as if it were a flag in a hurricane. He kept looking up at Billy and then back down again, afraid to actually take anything in case he was shouted at. His time on the streets had taught him how unpredictable people could be, seemingly kind with a smile, only to suddenly shout at him, chasing him away. Back when he was with his lady, the lovely woman, so kind, he knew nothing of the trials of life, but without her it had been a bumpy ride.

"Go on, boy," Billy said, unaware that Arthur was so wary, or why. Quickly he turned to the fridge again, wondering what else he might like.

Arthur dropped his head and pounced, like a lion seeking its prey. The meat tasted good, fresh and full of flavor. It was so different to what he had been eating when outside, scraps here and there, not to mention to odd morsels he had tasted since being in the house. This was fine, and so welcome. He knew then that the family were kind, so loving with their gifts of fine foods.

Billy took out a bowl full of newly made mashed potatoes. He had no idea what it would be for, but suspected Arthur might enjoy it. Quickly he dropped the plate, as he watched Arthur pull slices of meat, quickly gobbling it up, looking up occasionally to show how much he appreciated it.

As the mashed potato appeared beside him Arthur's eyes lit up, unable to comprehend the unfolding feast before him. He was many things, but certainly no fool, he wouldn't decline anything.

As the new dog ate, appearing to enjoy it all, Billy laughed. It was a sight to see, their new pet, new to the family, enjoying himself so much.

"Hold on, boy," Billy said, peering back into the fridge. "One more thing," he said, but Arthur took no notice, as if he would hold on a moment when such lovely food beckoned.

"Billy," a voice called. It was his mum, but he was too busy feeding the dog to stop and answer.

"Billy, where are you?" Nancy called again. No reply.

Nancy walked down the stairs, into the living room. There she saw Stan sat on the sofa, looking blankly at his newspaper, as if he were pretending to read it but in fact was actually asleep with his eyes open.

"Stan," Nancy called, but he continued to ignore her.

"Am I invisible?" Nancy asked herself. She looked at Abigail, as she sat watching the television.

"Have you seen Billy?" Nancy asked, looking at Abigail. She turned to looked at her mother, her eyes blank as if she were lost in her own world. The two looked at each other for a moment, like two strangers on a train platform, before Abigail once again resumed her television duties.

It was enough, as Nancy marched over, switching off the television.

"Hey," Abigail called, not too loud. She could say what she liked to Billy or her dad, but knew better than to raise her voice with her mother.

Nancy didn't wait for anything to be said, instead walking across to Stan, as she swiped her hand down on his newspaper. She had half imagined the paper dropping away and him not moving, eyes unblinking as if mind completely wiped. Instead Stan looked at her, raised eyebrows, a look of complete innocence.

"What's up, dear?" Stan asked, as polite as could be.

"Oh," Nancy said, doing her best to hold into her temper. She couldn't help but wonder why everyone else seemed to be off to happy land and yet she never could be. It was obvious she was the one in control, never able to do her own thing. It was the thing with responsibility, you could never take your eyes off what mattered, because you ended up being the only one acting responsible.

"Have you seen Billy?" Nancy asked again, spelling out her words.

"Oh," Stan replied, still not bothering to reply.

Nancy stood over him, looking at her husband intently, wondering what she could get away with in response if he didn't wake up from his dream.

"Maybe the dog ate him," Abigail replied. Nancy ignored her. She had been tempted to call her a typical teenager, which she wasn't quite, but knew it would be an excuse to rant about it, so didn't.

Finally something occurred in Stan's mind, about what was going on. "Where's Billy?" Stan asked, as if he had just thought of it. "Oh, he said he was going to feed the dog," Stan said, looking satisfied with himself that he had finally sparked his mind into offering something useful.

"Really," Nancy replied, turning to walk out. The moment she turned Stan felt the same sinking feeling he figured she might have. He quickly jumped up to follow.

Whatever it might be, it sounded like it might be fun, so Abigail followed, hoping for some payback for her annoying little brother.

Nancy walked into the kitchen, only for her jaw to drop to the floor. Stan looked over her shoulder as Abigail leaned sideways to see in. She couldn't help but smile.

Billy turned to see them all and smiled back. "I couldn't figure out what he might like, and didn't know what dogs ate, so I gave him a few things." He said, totally pleased with himself.

Laid out covering half of the kitchen floor were plates, bowls, packets, carriers, all sorts of foods, crisps, half-eaten meats and various foods chewed or completely gone. It was as if a hoard of ravenous but hungry giants had descended and scoffed the lot. There were no giants, only one very hungry dog, who was still licking the first plate of meat, now empty, because it had been so good.

Arthur stopped to look at them, wondering if there might be a drink to go with it. If meal times were like this every day, he was going to have a *very* good time.

Nobody spoke. Nancy wanted to, but what she was looking at was beyond words. As much as she wanted to scream, she could never scream loud enough to justify how she felt.

Abigail smiled, at first thinking of the trouble her brother might get into, but wanting as much as anything to laugh her head off.

"Billy," Stan said lowly, his voice trying to convey disappointment, but he did such a bad job of being stern Nancy looked at him as if he were simply mocking.

Silence befell them, as they all watched Arthur eat a week's food.

"Mum," Abigail said. Nancy couldn't bring herself to look at her daughter. She felt if she turned, or did anything, she might break into a thousand pieces.

"What, love?" Stan asked. Billy laughed, finding it funny his sister had said mum and his dad had replied.

"What's for tea?" Abigail replied, bursting out laughing. She didn't wait for the reply, instead quickly walking away, rushing upstairs to her room. The day had been an eventful one, and for her certainly a promise that the new addition to their family would be an interesting one.

"What are we going to do, Stan?" Nancy asked, feeling deflated.

"Clean up?" Stan replied, as always very functional his responses to problems.

"No, you know what I mean. Food," Nancy said, looking at him.

Arthur stopped eating long enough to look up, ears raised at the magic word.

"Chippy?" Stan asked, liking the idea of ordering in food.

There was nothing more to be said. Nancy walked over to Arthur, as he looked up at her, as excited as he had ever been.

"So, are there any things here he hasn't eaten, licked or nibbled?" Nancy asked, looking at her son. She was perfectly calm, fully aware that it hadn't been deliberate, or with malice. It was simply a very honest mistake.

"No, I think he likes everything," Billy replied, smiling at his mother. She could see the joy in his face, the sheer happiness. Nancy kneeled down, smiling gently back at him.

"I guess he doesn't handle a knife and fork very well, does he?" she asked, looking all the while at her son.

Billy laughed loudly. "No, Mum, I think he's a but mucky. He doesn't sit at the table either," he said, laughing ever more. He ran over to her, wrapping his arms around her as she pulled him in, resting her head against his.

It had been a mad day, and things seemed to be so crazy it was hard to keep a lid on their emotions, but together they knew one thing for sure: their new dog was going to be a lot of fun.

CHAPTER 4

"I guess we will have to go and do some shopping," Stan said, as he watched Nancy clean the kitchen.

Nancy looked up at him. "Yes, or you can go and I will stay on my knees here tidying up."

Stan scratched his head, not particularly fond of either option. He never enjoyed going out on a weekend, especially a Saturday when it was so busy, and worse still, so cold. Nancy had stopped cleaning up long enough to stare at him. Decisions, decisions. It was tough.

"Right, I will go get ready and we can go out," Stan finally said, pleased with himself for making a decision.

"I'll finish cleaning the kitchen, shall I? Then I'll join you shopping, and maybe in between I can massage your feet?" Nancy asked.

"Oh, now I like the sound of that," Stan said, smiling at her.

"I bet you do," Nancy said, as she stood up, throwing a cloth at him. "You clean here, I'll get dressed and go to the shops with Abigail. You look after Billy, and do a good job in here."

As Stan lifted his hand weakly to point out the problem with such an idea, mainly that he didn't like it, Nancy walked straight past him. All it needed was for her to pat him on the head and say *good boy* and he would have been put firmly in his place.

Feeling his ego a little punctured, Stan felt a need to assert himself. "Billy," he shouted. In the back of his mind an image struck him of what his son might be up to now, with the dog. He wasn't sure who he should be most worried about, the dog or his son.

"Yes, Dad," Billy shouted as he ran into the kitchen. Stan jumped, shocked, as Arthur chased after him, skidding on the newly wet floor before bumping into Billy. Both were out of breath, clearly having had a great deal of fun running around.

"Right," Stan said, hesitating, as both watched him intently. It was odd to him how quickly the two had created a bond, but as he thought about it he knew it shouldn't be strange, given the dog had been sleeping under his son's bed, for who knew how long.

"I think Arthur will probably need to go out into the garden to do his business. Can you get some shoes and a coat on and take him out?" Stan asked.

"Yep," Billy replied excitedly, turning to run away.

"Er," Stan said, wanting to say more, but his son was already gone. Arthur sat, looking at him, his tail shuffling side to side, as if waiting for something.

Stan shook his head, looking back at him, trying to fathom what the dog wanted. "If it's food you want, you've had enough."

Arthur shuffled slightly, closer, before gently lifting a paw towards him. The excited behavior had shifted, no longer panting so much, now he remained calm, looking intently at him.

"What?" Stan asked. There it was again, that same look from Arthur, a glint in his eyes, but a mystery behind them. Stan suspected whatever it was, he could never provide it.

"Billy," Stan shouted, at which Arthur quickly stood up and ran out. After a few moments both returned, Billy in his wellington boots, Arthur same as ever, excited by anything that happened.

"Ready, Dad," Billy said, as he struggled to pull on his gloves.

"Here, let me do it," Stan said, taking hold of a glove. Billy's fingers didn't match each place where they should be, but one by one he corrected them.

"Right, boys," Stan said, meaning them both. Billy laughed at the thought, as if Arthur was his brother. As much as it obviously pleased Billy that they had a new pet, a new dog, perhaps a brother, Stan felt a sense of unease over the situation. Things were fluid in his mind. The last thing he had ever imagined was getting a dog.

"Go do what has to be done, and Billy," Stan said hesitating.

"Yeah," Billy said, looking at his dad as if he were the only person in the world.

"Remember, when he does his business, you get to clear it up, and put it in the bin," Stan said, certain of what was going to happen.

"Yes, Dad, no problem, we'll do it," Billy replied, his mind clearly not on the matter anymore.

"Walkies," Billy called, looking at Arthur. Before Stan could say a word his son had run out, followed quickly by Arthur as the two ran down the stairs.

As Billy and Arthur ran, Nancy walked past. "Make sure you shut the door, it's freezing out," she shouted. Obviously the door would remain open, it always did.

"Come on, boy," Billy called, but he had no need to, Arthur would stay with him come what may. As Billy opened the door a sweep of snow swept in, as the white skies opened up, showering the landscape with a thick quilt of white.

"Wow, it's snowing heavy," Billy said as he stepped out into the laden patio. Arthur cautiously followed him, immediately aware of the bitter cold. He had grown accustomed quickly to the warmth indoors, and really didn't want to go back out again. All the while, as he walked, one paw in front of the other, slowly, he wondered if he might go out and never be allowed back in again.

Billy had no understanding of his emotions, instead rolling up a snowball. He threw it, no interest in where it might land, simply giggling at the fun of it.

As the ball flew, Arthur instinctively ran for it, trying to jump, only too late as it splattered against the shed door.

Again Billy rolled another, only waiting a moment, to catch Arthur's attention. Both stood looking at one another, as Arthur hunched down, ready to spring. The snowball flew, again too fast, as it hit the ground before Arthur could react.

"Hold on, boy, here we go," Billy said, rolling one more. This time he flicked it up gently, closer. Arthur jumped up and at it, like a kangaroo hopping in the air, grabbing at it with his mouth. It was bitterly cold as he bit into it, but so much fun. Billy laughed loudly. It was a great day, for them both.

Again Billy picked up a snowball, throwing it gently at Arthur, as it splashed against his muzzle, Arthur bit it still, sending white powder all over. Again, another in the air, only this time Arthur jumped so high it seemed like magic to Billy. Arthur grabbed the snow, breaking it quickly with his mouth, shaking his head abruptly as he reacted to the bitter chill in his mouth.

Billy laughed as Arthur panted, a crazy moment of merriness, such fun, so happy together.

"You're amazing, Arthur," Billy shouted, at which Arthur took one look at him, ran to a corner, sniffed around and back to the center of the garden, before lowering himself ready to do his business.

"Oh," Billy said, not having seen properly how a dog works in such ways before.

Arthur glanced over at him, as the mass of food did its thing, leaving a mess that no one would be able to deal with.

"Mum," Billy shouted, watching the dog do his thing. It wasn't at all what he had expected.

"Eurgh," Billy said to himself, as he struggled to watch what was going on.

Instead of his mother, it was Stan who poked his head out. He looked over at Billy, then to where he was looking, as Arthur went about what came most natural.

"Ugh, Dad," Billy said, sneering.

"What did you expect, that he would climb on the toilet and read the paper?" Stan asked. Billy laughed, but it was no laughing matter.

"Yeah, but why is it so, you know," Billy asked, unable to bring himself to say it.

"Watery?" Stan asked, without flinching. He hadn't thought much about it, but given what Arthur had been eating, the response was hardly a shock.

"Yeah," Billy said, looking away. He held his nose, struggling to deal with the fallout.

"Well, there you go, that's what happens when you have a dog. You get to clean it up," Stan insisted.

"Why do I have to clean it up?" Billy asked.

"You fed him, you clean it up." It never occurred to Stan that he was being harsh, or why he was being the way he was.

"Come in, Billy, Dad will do it."

Stan turned suddenly to see Nancy stood there, in her coat, with Abigail alongside her.

"Me," Stan said, thinking to argue about it, but instantly deciding not to, given the look on her face. He could see she was not best pleased about things, so decided not to push it.

"Yes, you," Nancy said, stepping out.

"Good luck with that, Dad," Abigail said, not daring to look.

Arthur was busy scraping his hind legs in the snow, trying to cover his business, before doing the smart thing and running back into the house. He didn't wait for anyone to complain, and if they had he fully intended to run inside, and hide if necessary.

Billy took his lead, shuffling in the snow as it flurried around his boots. "Good luck, Dad," he said, smiling at his father and mirroring his sister. He never would have said a word if his sister hadn't been so forthright. He wasn't so daring as she. Not yet.

Nobody else spoke, as Nancy and Abigail walked out and through the gate. The snow was falling heavier than ever as Billy walked back into the house, threw off his wellington boots, dropped his coat to the floor and ran upstairs.

Stan remained rooted to the spot, by the front door, still in his pajamas and slippers. He began to shiver, wondering just who was in charge in the house, before accepting it was everyone but him. He grabbed a coat from the rack in the hall, decided to leave his slippers on and stepped out. A shovel nearby would do, as it had quickly turned white, it became obvious to him; it was going to be a long day.

Inside was warm, even with the door open. It was one of the good things about having a house on three floors, where the cold from outside was often masked by higher floors and rising heat. Though it was only afternoon, the exertions of the day had taken their toll on Billy, as he felt his energy diminishing. He felt tired, and not a little hungry, but for all that all he could think of was their new dog. It seemed unreal to think about it, that they would even have him. All they had ever been told was no pets, with endless excuses, so now it was amazing, impossible to even dream about, their own dog.

"Arthur," Billy called, wondering where he might be. As much as he wanted to call him, his stomach was calling too. He walked along the hall, into the kitchen, looking around without actually opening any doors or cupboards. It all seemed like too much work, given his mother wasn't in and his father was scooping up, the thought of actually preparing his own food was too much to do. Quickly he glanced around to see if Arthur was there; he wasn't, so off he went, continuing to search.

Billy walked into the living room, to see the floor covered in cuddly toys, mostly his own. He felt so tired his eyes played tricks on him, as if they were all little Arthur's, waiting to be played with. The sofa looked so inviting, he wanted to put the television on and jump into a nice comfy chair, to just drift off into an aimless sleep. Usually he would, but not this time; this time he couldn't stop thinking about Arthur. It would be ace to simply cuddle up with him.

Back out into the hall he went, missing the lovely warmth of the living room already. He looked out the back window, small but enough to see the back garden. There was a slender man in his pajamas, bending over with a shovel, scooping up muddy snow, not looking particularly happy. Billy made a mental note to himself: don't rush to be an adult, and when you are one, maybe don't get a dog.

"Arthur," Billy whispered, wondering if he would come running. He waited, holding his breath. Nobody, just silence. He shivered, feeling the difference in temperature. It wasn't great, so decided to go look upstairs for him. Deep down he figured Arthur wouldn't be hungry, not after that feast, so he might be hiding somewhere.

"Arthurrrrr," Billy whispered, a little louder now. Still no sound. He went up the stairs, looking at first in the bathroom, before realizing no sensible dog would be seen in such a place, especially after that bath. He chuckled to himself as he imagined the scenes from earlier, as Arthur had jumped out and ran around like a fool.

"Here, boy," Bill called, gently, but nothing. He walked along to his room, on the off chance that he might have gone back in there. Looking around all he could see were a mess of toys and clothes all over the floor.

The quilt on his bed was in a large messy pile, his pillows looking like they had been run over by a truck, but no signs up their new dog. Billy felt his heart skip a beat, at the thought that Arthur might have got out and run off again. Surely not, he thought, even a dog isn't that daft.

The warmth from the radiator filled the room, reminding him of the difference as he moved around, it was lovely, so inviting, calling to him to drift off into slumber town. As much as he wanted to, he couldn't do it without knowing about that little brown pooch.

"Please, Arthur," Billy called, louder now thinking maybe he should just shout, right at the top of his lungs, but then Dad might hear and if Arthur had done something else that was wrong, well, anything could happen.

Billy slumped down on his floor, grabbing at one of the plastic soldiers on its side. He threw it, watching it bounce off a wall, back to the floor and nearby. As he looked, he saw a small pair of eyes looking back at him, from under his bed. It was Arthur, back there, where he felt safe. His tail flicked up a little, as if a sheepish sign of hello, but in reality he was just tired, and half asleep.

"Ohhhh," Billy whispered, feeling a spread of joy. He smiled at Arthur, watching him intently, as the small eyes glittered and blinked, before closing again, passing off into restless sleep.

It was perfect. The room was warm, so quiet. They had been out and played in the amazing snow, and Arthur had enjoyed a cheeky feast. Now they were together, in their own room, theirs. Arthur had gone back to sleep, in the place Billy knew he belonged. Quickly he jumped up onto his bed, dragging what he could of his covers over him, resting his head on a mountain which used to be a pillow. Together they drifted off, ready to dream of adventures to come.

CHAPTER FIVE

"You look a bit wet," Nancy said as she pushed the gate open. The snow had eased but still fell mildly. Everywhere was covered in inches of it, including the garden where Stan was trying to clear.

"Thank you," Stan said trying to sound sarcastic, but instead sounding annoyed.

"I thought you might have cleared the path, Dad," Abigail said, struggling to walk while holding several carrier bags.

Stan looked around, to see his handiwork. As fast as he had cleared snow, more had fallen in its place. He was soaked. By the time he thought of putting on a coat, it was too late anyway. He had done so much for so long, he was both shivering and sweating at the same time.

"Thank you both, I have done my best," Stan said, leaning against his snow shovel.

"Oh, dear," Nancy said, half mocking, playfully. "Look at you though, you're going to get ill. Come on in and forget about the garden."

Stan looked at her, as his wet hair dripped down his face. He looked over at Abigail. "Your turn to clean up after the dog next," he said, throwing the shovel onto the snow covered lawn.

"No chance," Abigail said, trudging over to the door. She leaned in, nudging the handle open, before crashing in with the bags of food. "It's your dog, you can clean up after him," she said, before disappearing inside.

It was an odd thing to hear, not the least because it was his young daughter saying it, but also because of what she had said: it was his dog. He hadn't wanted a dog, and he certainly didn't want his mother's dog. He wanted to say more, but held his tongue.

"Where's Billy? I thought he would be out here playing in the snow, and with Arthur," Nancy said, slowly walking around the garden

Stan followed her, only now realizing how cold he was. "Not seen him, I guess he's inside watching television."

"Or eating what's left in the house, with the dog," Nancy replied, realizing it wasn't the best of jokes, given what had happened.

"Billy," Nancy called. She knew what he was like, often half-engrossed in some cartoon or other on television. If not then he would be in his room, playing with toys. She could only imagine what he might get up to, now he had a dog to play with. The mess, the horror, and the other mess. Only one person would clean it up.

"Have you not seen him?" Nancy asked again as they walked up the stairs. Nancy struggled with carrier bags of food as Stan walked behind her. She looked back at him, wondering if he might take a bag or two, but given his state, looking as if he had fallen in a barrel of water, she decided not to push it.

"No," was all Stan said, shaking his head. The warmth inside was welcome, reminding him of how foolish he had been.

"I guess you'll go get changed, and then we can put food away," Nancy said, wanting to be sarcastic, but deciding now wasn't the time.

"Or we could just go give it all to the dog and get it over with," Stan said quietly as they both entered the hallway. Nancy laughed, turning to kiss him on the cheek. She loved him for his humor, and his sense of balance in all things. No matter how bad things got, he would never panic, and would never raise his voice. It was times like that which reminded her why she loved him.

"Maybe go drop the bags in the kitchen and we can go up and look for him," Stan said.

"OK," Nancy replied, quickly taking the food and following him back.

"Abigail," Nancy called.

"Yes," Abigail replied, clearly coming from the living room.

"Is Billy with you, or Arthur?" Nancy asked, peering around the door.

"Nope, not here," Abigail replied. She was sat on the floor, lost in her own world, much like her brother, only for very different reasons.

"He's not in the kitchen, I just checked. I guess upstairs," Nancy said, which was welcome news to Stan, as he shivered, even with the heating full on.

Together they went up again, as Nancy listened. She had expected Billy to be running around with Arthur, making mayhem and loving it all. Instead there was silence, nothing at all.

"I bet he's fallen asleep on his bed," Stan said, heading straight for their bedroom to get dressed.

"No doubt," Nancy said, as she walked into Billy's room. The first thing she saw was a large mound that used to be a quilt. It was lifted up like a cloth mountain, and beside it a pillow that looked every bit the same, only smaller.

33

"Hey," Nancy said, gently nudging the quilt, expecting Billy to be curled up in a ball, wrapped up neatly in it. The quilt fell open, cold and empty.

Nancy looked up and around the room, realizing he wasn't there.

"Found him?" Stan asked, having dressed in a baggy t-shirt and equally slack jogging bottoms. He held a pair of socks in his hand, knowing he was going to be cold for the rest of the day.

"No, he's not here," Nancy said, for the first time feeling concerned. She struggled with being concerned and annoyed. She was used to her son being wayward, but couldn't quite bring herself to say anything reproachful.

Stan sniffed. "I think I might have a cold coming on," he said. Nancy pulled a face at him in response.

"Oh, do you have a cold coming on too?" Stan asked.

"No, I'm pulling a face because we can't find our son and the first thing you think of is how you're feeling," Nancy said, shaking her head.

"Ah," Stan said, immediately beginning to look around, making it obvious with his wild gestures. Nancy watched as he mimicked Billy, running around like a mad man, looking in cupboards, throwing himself to the floor and looking at the carpet, generally acting up.

Nancy laughed, unable to stop herself. It was too much effort to be in a bad mood, and the wrong time to be doing it anyway.

"Found him under the carpet, have we?" Nancy asked, smiling at him.

Stan stopped what he was doing and looked up at her. "No, I have no idea," he said, his voice trailing off as something caught his attention.

"Oh, and now I guess cat has got your tongue," Nancy said, stood hands on hips.

"Not quite," Stan hesitated, as he edged closer to Billy's room, all the while on his knees.

"Are we all going barking mad now?" Nancy asked, deciding to get into the same mood everyone else seemed to be in.

Stan ignored her, creeping into Billy's room. "Guess what I found, under a little boy's bed," Stan asked, staring intently.

"No, Arthur isn't back under his bed is he?" Nancy asked. She bent over, before slowly easing herself to the floor. It was never her favorite place to be, let alone while surrounded by toys and clothes.

As she sat she lowered herself further, to look into the darkness underneath. She could just about see Arthur's head, poking above what looked like a towel, wrapped around a small cuddly toy.

"I guess he likes it under there," Nancy said, wondering what to do.

Stan sat up, looking directly at her.

"What?" Nancy asked, surprised by the look on his face.

"Look again, closer," he said, without a hint of a smile, but his voice betrayed him; he had seen more.

Nancy looked, staring into the dark, seeing Arthur, as he rested his head again, eyes closing as he drifted off. He breathed in gently, expanding his chest, ready to sigh, but as he did he lifted up a little, just enough to give away the hidden little boy, his arms wrapped around him, fast asleep as if this new dog were a comfy, fluffy pillow.

"Oh," Nancy said, pushing her hands to her mouth, as if she might otherwise cry about it. Stan remained quiet, knowing anything he might say would ruin the moment.

The two looked at each other, smiling. They knew they couldn't leave them permanently like that, but for now they could just enjoy it.

"I guess when tea is ready we can give them a shout. I bet they come running then," Nancy said, laughing quietly. Stan nodded, before standing quickly up. He lowered his hand, helping up his wife, as the two left, carefully pulling the door to.

Arthur opened his eyes a moment, looking out to where they had been. He felt Billy's warmth, and all the affection that came with him. He had found a new friend, someone to love, and perhaps with him a new home. Time   would   tell.

CHAPTER SIX

Monday. The worst day of the week, off out to school, off out to work. Mornings. The worst time of the day, getting up, out of a nice warm bed, getting dressed and hoping it isn't too cold, rushing around, trying to eat, knowing you have to go out.

"Can I stay off?" Billy asked, looking at Arthur, as he looked back, feeling confused by all the fuss.

"No, love, you have to go to school. So does Abigail, and Dad and I have to go to work," Nancy said, wrapping his coat around him while fastening buttons.

Billy coughed. "I don't feel well," he offered.

"Hey, maybe he has a cold, like I had on Saturday?" Stan replied.

"Maybe he's got man flu, like you always get?" Abigail interrupted, taking a drink from the fridge and placing it in her bag.

"Hey," Billy called, loudly.

"Oh, I guess your throat is instantly better," Abigail said, goading him.

"No," Billy croaked, suddenly ill again.

"Sorry, love, you're going to school," Nancy insisted, passing his school bag to him.

"I'm off out," Stan said, quickly pecking Nancy on the cheek. Before she had a chance to look up he was gone, down the stairs and away.

All the while, sat in a corner, watching all the commotion was Arthur. It was something he had never seen before. He couldn't help but wonder if he might be wrapped up in a coat, or be asked to leave. Quietly he shook, feeling deeply uneasy that his fine weekend in the warmth was about to come to an end, and once again he would be back on the street.

"Bye, Arthur," Billy cried, rubbing his head gently before walking off.

"Oh don't be silly, why are you crying?" Nancy asked as she walked behind him.

"Because I miss Arthur," Billy replied, wiping his nose on his coat sleeve.

"Oh, come on, it's fine," Nancy said, hugging him and nudging him to move faster at the same time. They were late, which was the last thing she needed.

"Are you ready," Nancy began to call.

"Yes, Mum, I'm ready, I'm leaving," Abigail called. She had half a mind to wait til they had gone and then slink back into bed, but she knew mock exams were running, and couldn't take the time off. She glanced at Arthur as she walked down the hall. Immediately he looked up at her, his ears pricked up, eyes wide, as if she were his last line of hope, the one that would save him from the streets. He knew full well she could also be the one to kick him out, to chase him back out into the snow, but as always he was a dog of hope, and until it happened he would, as ever, be happy.

"I don't know what you're looking for, but whatever it is, I don't have it," Abigail said, taking a biscuit from the counter.

Just as she was about to walk off, ready to leave, she stopped and turned to look at him. "Mutt," she said, at which his ears dropped, as if he had been told off and he knew it.

Instead of being angry, she leaned over, wrapped an arm around him, and hugged him for all she was worth. Quite why she had done it, even she didn't know, it was simply an act of instinct. Even Arthur was confused, not having had any attention from her since he had been discovered.

"I guess you're not so bad after all," she said, standing up. The moment she stood, all fond sentiments disappeared as she quickly became aware that her uniform was covered in dog fur.

"Arthur," she shouted, quickly wiping it off as she walked down the hall. For his part he ran, frightened by the sudden change of heart. Off he went, running up the stairs, down to the end of the hall, only to find the door closed. As he turned around he looked one way, to Billy's room, closed, to the other room, closed, everywhere closed to him.

Back down the stairs he ran, back to the kitchen, to see he was alone, before heading into the living room. There he stopped, finally realizing he was genuinely alone again.

He panted quickly, out of breath for his unusual burst. He looked out of the window, seeing the heavy snow fall, as people walked to and fro, and cars passed. He remembered the ice cold nights, curled up in a ball, shivering so much he could hardly sleep. Now, in the house, the heating had been left on, radiators emanating heat, it was so nice it didn't feel real.

Always at the back of his mind was the thought that at any moment someone would come in and shoo him away, tell him that he had made a mistake, that he had to get out. Of course it never happened, not this time, but it wouldn't take away the fear. Nothing would take that away again.

Still, he was free again, to roam a little. There was only one place he was going to go, it called to him, like a whisper in the night which offered him the kind of peace that could only come from a full tummy.

Off Arthur trotted on his merry way, free as a bird, into the kitchen, his sanctuary. He stopped a moment, as if savoring the possibilities. There was the counter, going all the way along the back wall, or the white big box thing which he remembered that tasty chicken from, and then there was the table, often full of food, but perhaps not right then. He looked around while stood in the doorway, sniffing the air for any signs of the right scent. For the moment all he could smell was his own fur, smelling like strawberries after that water in the tub, and on Abigail's bed. No matter, he would lick it all off and be clean soon enough.

Walking slowly around he sensed there was no food anywhere, none on the counter to jump up to, the white box thing was tightly closed, and the table appeared empty. He was out of luck, abandoned for food in his hour of need.

Then his nose caught something, an unusual scent, one that reminded him of something from the time before, back when someone else loved him so much he felt like a puppy every day.

He sniffed and sniffed, until his nose dragged him around to a corner on the other side of the room, down on the floor. There lay two bowls, one white, one yellow, one clearly full of water, but the other seemed to have something piled in it.

Whatever it was, even if it wasn't food, given his nature he was certainly going to give it a try. As he stood over it, he noticed it was a reasonable pile of brown bits and pieces.

Arthur stopped a moment, wondering whether to go ahead, or if he did would someone come crashing in, shouting at him for doing wrong? Would he have to go running like a fool all over the house, trying to get away from the anger? Did it belong to him, or did it belong to Mr. and Mrs. Angry? His head told him walk away, be smart, don't touch the trap. His stomach didn't agree, always seeming to be empty and in need of a new refill.

Arthur, being the smart dog he was, decided he would be good, he would walk away and go back to sleep. The thought lasted barely two seconds as he gave in to temptation and began shoving his muzzle into the pile. At first it seemed a little off, not like the lovely meat he had eaten in recent days, more dry, but still tasty. Once he had a huge mouthful any thoughts of who it belonged to went right out of the door, as he munched away like a cow eating the cud.

Still, there was always the chance someone would come in and order him to get away, which of course was a good excuse to eat more and eat faster. So he did. Kibble spilled all over the floor, as if it were trying to escape. Arthur scrambled to mop it up, as if his mouth were a giant kibble vacuum, where nothing must be left alone. It was his job, no, his duty, to clean up every single piece, then return to the bowl and continue his crunchy feast.

It wasn't the best, but it would do, for now. He munched and crunched and ate until the bowl was empty. Then he licked the bowl, looked up, felt sad because it was all gone, and licked it again, hard this time in case more came out.

Arthur looked up, sniffing a moment in case he had missed something, then became aware of how heavy he felt. He looked around, noticing a huge biscuit-laden bulge in his stomach. It was a sign that new dog owners perhaps should know how much to feed a dog, because dogs like Arthur certainly didn't have a kibble *off* button.

Finally he burped, releasing air due to the fact that he had eaten so quickly he had swallowed a lot of it.

He was happy, pleased with himself, for finding the secret treasure, the hidden feast, the food that was his, rightly so. Next up would be a place to sleep, and it seemed he was spoiled for choice with this one.

After a deep and enjoyable drink from the bowl of water, which for some reason splashed all over the floor and all around, Arthur walked away. He felt like someone had strapped a large bag to his tummy, he was so full, as his stomach sloshed and swung around. He felt like collapsing there and then, rolling over and having the world's best sleep. Of course he wouldn't, because he loved his new-found comfort too much. It reminded him of home, wherever and whatever that was, he no longer felt so sure of it.

Arthur walked slowly into the living room, felt the heat from the radiators and immediately walked nearer, ready to curl up in a ball next to it. He sat, looking around, feeling an odd sensation, one that he hadn't felt for a while. Before, he had no time to think about it, because he was so busy trying to survive, and to escape so many people who clearly didn't love him. Now he had time to stop and think, now that it was quiet, it reminded him of what had changed, how much he had lost, and what might happen to him next. Sitting there, it just wasn't right. He was alone, and that was the worst feeling in the world for him. Even if they couldn't be with him, he needed something to remind him that they were there, or had been, to give hope that once again they would come back.

It was a given, what he had to do, so off he went, back slowly up the stairs, along the hall, and to the little boy's room. He nudged the door, slightly at first, then more, until he managed to push it open. The air was different, all childlike smells, the clothes on the floor with his scent, the natural odor which felt right. Darkness under the bed welcomed him, as place to be, a home, until they came back, and once again they would all be happy as he slept, not so silently this time, but snored, under Billy's bed.

CHAPTER SEVEN

The snow had stopped, but the skies remained dark, full of foreboding clouds, threatening to unleash a storm at any moment. As Stan drove, his mind mirrored that of the skies, but for all that occurred around him, he only had thoughts for one thing. It was the day, the one day he had been dreading the most, but couldn't forget. Nancy reminded him, picked at him, nudged him, reminded him he had to, it was the right thing to do.

As he drove along the road through town, slush either side as cars crawled through the snow, he continued as if on autopilot. He was no fool, still aware of his obligations on the road, to himself and his family and others driving nearby, but still the distraction was intense.

Finally he pulled up into the reserved parking space, slowly opened his door, and felt his heart beat faster and harder than he could ever recall. Each step he took towards the house seemed to tap in time with his heart.

Pushing the key into the door took effort, as if he were too weak to even do the mundane things. In his mind it was obvious he had grown into the habit of living life, looking forward so much that what had happened before in his life no longer seemed real, no longer seemed to matter. It was a bad habit to hold onto, but to him it sometimes seemed to be the only way to keep going. Of course he would never tell his children such, but he could never hide it from Nancy.

Stan stamped his feet, throwing off the remnants of snow from his shoes. His socks were wet and his feet cold, but it seemed so unimportant, he simply ignored it. On any other day he would be running upstairs, grabbing new socks, warming his feet, perhaps a change of shoes, but today he didn't care. His emotions were switched off.

The place was silent, but warm and welcoming. He didn't need to see the faces of his children or his loving wife to appreciate that it was a part of him. The silence was different though, as much in his mind as in reality, surrounded by a blanket of quiet, where all he could hear was his own heartbeat. It seemed in rhythm with his self, uneven and unsure, even if not actually there.

As if on rails Stan walked along, dripping wet onto the carpet but uncaring. He walked up the stairs, heading into the kitchen. Ignoring the remnants of kibble on the floor and splashed water he opened a wall cupboard in the corner, before taking out a new dog lead and harness that Nancy had bought on her shop.

"Arthur," Stan called. It wasn't loud, enough so that it could be heard through the house. Without waiting he walked back along the hall and down the stairs to the door. As if a bond had already been created between them, Arthur quickly moved out from his hiding place and ran along the landing and down. He stood in the hall at the opposite end of the kitchen, uncertain of where he was being called from, so waited. It wasn't the voice of a child, or even Nancy, it was a man, and certain enough to know it was from someone in charge.

"Here," was all Stan said, at which Arthur once again made his way quickly down the stairs. There he saw Stan opening the door, walking out. Arthur followed, looking up at him occasionally. As uncertain as he was, he could still feel they were going for a walk.

Stan stopped a moment to look at him. From this Arthur could see the sadness in his eyes, and once again the old fears returned. In that short single pause, they both looked at one another, wary of what the other might do. Could it really be over, after so much fun, being cleaned, being fed, and finally being loved? After all that, could they really say goodbye to him like this? After his experiences on the street, Arthur already knew the answer.

"Come on, put this on," Stan said, pulling the cardboard backing off the harness. It was designed to go over the neck and around the shoulders, black in color, and adjustable for comfort. Arthur had only ever worn a simple collar, so knew little of what to expect. The lead was a long metal chain, with a leather strap for a handle. It clinked as Stan moved around, making Arthur jump.

In that instant, just before the harness went over his head, Arthur wondered if now was the time to run. Would he end up on another cage? Would he end up in a place alone again, unwanted? It seemed so much likely. There was nowhere to run, with the gate closed. He could run into the house, maybe hide. Perhaps if he did they might go all soft and laugh, as they seemed to have done before, but probably not.

Arthur's ears dropped low as he bowed his head. At first he tried to resist the harness going over, but it was more accident than by design. It was obvious what was coming, and although in the last he had been ready to run and resist, to get what he wanted, he had been so happy until now that he no longer had the strength.

Stan tightened the harness so that it was firmly in place, then looked at him.

"I know, boy, I don't like it either, but it has to be done," he said, sounding as sad as Arthur felt.

"Come on," Stan said, gently tugging at the lead. Arthur reluctantly followed as they walked down the end of the garden. It was the first time that he had been away from the house and garden since he discovered the safety under the bed, and couldn't help but feel nervous. Without even being aware of it he began to shiver, slightly at first and more as they walked away.

Through the gate a cold wind blew past, out in the alley, as if in time with their journey. If he were to be back on the streets again it would be a hard time, worse than anything he had ever experienced.

Stan walked up to a car, opened the back door and stood looking at Arthur. "Come on, jump in," he said, waving his arm to do so. Arthur looked at him, not wanting to make eye contact, out of sheer surprise over what was happening.

"Come on, now, please," Stan snapped. It was unlike him, usually so polite and calm. Stan tugged the lead again, pulling it closer to the car, making it obvious he had no choice. Finally he leaped up, onto the back seat. Stan leaned in, lifted a long black lead which was attached to the seat belt clip, locking him in place.

The door slammed, again making Arthur jump. It was silent for a short time as Stan walked around to the driver's side of the car. In that moment Arthur felt as low as he ever had, not helped by the man in charge of him right then hardly speaking to him.

Once in, Stan turned on the engine and leaned around to look at Arthur. Quickly his ears pricked up, but back down again, showing just how confused he had become.

"This won't take long, and then we can get you settled," Stan said, before looking back and continuing to drive. Arthur didn't understand the words, but he knew enough now about human nature, and how people spoke to know that what was coming wasn't going to be good.

The car backed out into the main road as broken snow slushed around them, before powering away. Arthur looked out of the window feeling curious, as the streets flew past, he saw things he remembered from his days outside, the building being knocked down was gone, just a metal fence around it. Across the way was a large roundabout, filled with cars, reminding him of his close calls as he ran, not to mention the huge bus that he nearly got run over by. In any other circumstances he would have been thrilled to see it all again, but that deep down sense of dread, that he was going to be alone again, ate away at him.

Stan drove alone, down the road past Sainsbury's, through the first set of lights and along past various high-rise buildings. The tension in the car was obvious as Arthur kept looking up, his ears up as his instincts were to be excited, only to drop again as he was reminded of what was happening.

Finally they pulled up at a small set of traffic lights and stopped. Along one whole side of the road were high black railings, with large white concrete pillars beside huge open gates. On the other side was a prime white building, with bright letters above. Outside stood a man, dressed scruffily. He wore oil-stained jeans and a baggy hoodie. His hair was long and dirty, and his face was covered in a long straggly beard. He was stood holding a drink, staring directly at Arthur. To Arthur he looked like the man who had chained him outside, and shown little care for him. It was an uneasy moment, until the man turned and walked back inside.

Instead of driving off as the lights changed to green, Stan turned the car suddenly right, passing slowly through the gates, into the open area. He stopped a moment, opened his side window and looked out. He nodded at a figure in a small building inside before turning right once again, driving down a narrow road. This was it, such a short distance away, before they would get out and he would be handed over, back into the arms of another stranger, or worse, someone he had known from before but didn't ever want to see again.

The car pulled up to a stop, as Stan opened his door. He hesitated, looking out, as if he too was unsure of what to do. Arthur felt a sense of hope, something he was naturally inclined to do, but lately felt reluctant to give in to.

Without speaking Stan finally stood up, allowing his door to close again. He walked around the back of the car as Arthur followed his every move. The snowfall had eased up, finally allowing sunshine to break through. The boot lid of the car lifted up as Stan leaned in. Finally he slammed it shut, before coming around for Arthur. This was it, the moment, ready to give life to the sickening sense of sadness and loss which was obvious between them.

Arthur's door opened slowly, at which he leaned out a little, trying to see as much of what was going on, as if he could see a lot and be ready for anything that might occur. Of course, even he couldn't be ready for what would happen.

Stan looked at him again, his eyes reddened, his cheeks flushed, as he too shivered. It was a sad state of affairs between them, but one that was unavoidable. Without saying a word he leaned in, unclipping Arthur, before taking a hold of his lead and pulling gently. It was at that moment when Arthur spotted Stan holding something in his hand, and noticed the heavy scent coming from it. Arthur sniffed, as he loved to do, head bobbing cutely as he tried to discover what it was that was wrapped so well.

Stan tugged the lead again and Arthur followed, standing up and jumping out, down onto the tarmac outside.

Surrounding them were well-mown grass areas, in a field of short but similar concrete blocks. Each had flowers in front of them, offering a confusing array of smells, wrapped in a distinctive show of color. Here and there walked a few passersby, some stood unable to hold onto their emotions.

Stan closed the door and began to walk. Arthur followed. His first instinct when he saw the open space was to run, but with the lead on, being held tightly, he had no choice but to follow. Off they went, at first quickly as Stan walked ahead, but as they progressed the walk slowed almost to a crawl.

Although the skies had cleared, leaving a canvas of deepest blue, it remained bitterly cold. When they walked occasionally on the verges the grass underfoot remained crisp, crackling with the frigidity of the frost. Snow lay around but had been cleared by visitors and staff alike, as if to provide a semblance of life where none existed.

The air felt light and clear, as if walking on a mountaintop, but with each step something else married around them, like a soft quilt of emotion wrapping around them, cosseting them both.

Together they walked around a twisting path, ahead to an open area covered by several tall trees. The moment they took the turn Stan began to cough, as if he were struggling to breathe. Arthur hesitated, feeling the man's reluctance, beginning to share his apprehension. It became like walking in treacle, each step mired in a febrile emotion.

Finally Arthur stopped. Pulling heavily on his lead, refusing to continue. It was as much a surprise to himself as it was to Stan. Even he had no idea why he had reacted in such a manner, so out of character, but something had stopped him, like a silent scream. Arthur's instincts kicked in, like a whirlwind sweeping around him, a hidden voice telling him he shouldn't go any further.

Stan was in no mood to argue. In part he didn't want to go either, but his conscience ate at him, told him he had obligations, some things just had to be done.

"What's up, Arthur?" Stan asked, turning to look at him. It was a pointless question, but in his mind he was only a dog, but even if he was, it was clear they shared a common doubt. Dogs couldn't speak, but often they didn't need to, because a look would say it all, and right then and there the way they looked at one another said everything. Stan leaned over, realizing then how weak he felt, but he had time to share a thought with their new dog, her dog.

Placing the flowers to the ground, Stan placed two hands on Arthur's head, for the first time rubbing his ears, at which Arthur sat, closing his eyes.

"Come on," Stan whispered. "Just a minute, and then we can go."

Finally they both stood with Stan collecting the flowers. It was as if a degree of unspoken agreement had been shared between them. Stan turned slowly, looked ahead, and walked again. This time Arthur followed, having no desire to. His instincts were fine, telling him what was coming. It showed him things he had no desire to know, an understanding of grief and loss which few animals could ever comprehend. Arthur could.

Together they walked up onto the grass, moving between headstones, ignoring the others, so much and so many. Finally Stan stopped, looking uneasily at one recently laid stone. He barely looked at the inscription, but this was the right place.

Arthur sniffed at the air, feeling a sense of sickness in his stomach. It was natural to him, but still his instincts were all over, like a radar in a magnetic storm. Only now he had no compass, if he wanted to run he couldn't escape the truth of why they were there. This time there would be no attempts at freedom, he would be where he needed to, because he had a family, and deep down understood that much. It was all so different, but even though only a dog, he still had expectations, and for all his quiet mind, he still had a care for Stan.

Without speaking Stan laid the flowers onto the grave, opening up the bunch, but no matter what, he never cried. Not this time, not yet.

Arthur stood a little, walking over to Stan, as if to nudge him. He could feel the well of emotion, and knew why. It was something they shared, because she was worth it, she was that good, though Stan couldn't say it.

That was enough. It was difficult, like pressing skin against a hot flame, because it confronted things that Stan never wanted to. For Arthur, it was a link to his past, but one to his future too. It was as if his mind were blank, for all the answers he had, he still felt confused.

"Let's go home, boy," Stan said, again slowly walking away.

Arthur recognized that word, *home*. For all the difficulties of that moment, that word said so much to him. He was allowed to imagine coming full circle, back to where he had started. As much as Arthur felt that, the difference in how Stan behaved proved difficult to come to terms with. It was an unanswered question, one that would not go away.

Without saying anything more, Stan opened the car, moved Arthur in to the back seat, got in and drove off. He returned to the house, saw Arthur inside, and left again.

Arthur stood looking out of the glass through the bottom of the door, watching the man go. No emotion now, no tears, no words. Arthur felt it though, like a heaving dam waiting to break. There would be time.

CHAPTER EIGHT

By the time Nancy finished work the snow had begun to fall heavily again. Roads were slow moving, and paths treacherous as ever. Though she worked short days because of the kids, it was still challenging dealing with it all; work, kids, a new dog, not to mention her husband and his response to things. For now all she could think about was getting indoors and warming up.

As she walked across the snow-covered garden she felt thankful for not working far from where they lived. The house was on the edge of town, and as such she could walk to places. It was never ideal walking in bad weather, but at least better than driving in such snow.

Fumbling for her keys, Nancy felt an icy chill down her spine, as she wondered how long the peace would last before the children came in and lit the place up.

All thoughts of peace disappeared the moment she got in, as she spotted a shirt dragged across the floor, obviously one of Stan's. As she looked at it, dragged out as if in a long line, laying there on the cold but not so clean floor, she wondered what was going on. Any questions she had were answered in just that moment, as Arthur came crashing down the stairs. She looked at him as he bounded down, for the briefest moment as if he hadn't even noticed she was there. He stopped, his hind legs half up the stairs, his front paws resting on the cold floor, panting away.

Just as he was about to run again, Nancy closed the door, slowly enough, but still it clicked as it did. Arthur jumped, turning quickly to see her. As she looked, she could see he had something in his mouth, as he struggled to breathe while still holding onto it.

"What?" Nancy began to ask, just as she realized he was holding a sock in his mouth. Arthur licked his mouth, pushing the sock away until it fell on the floor. He looked at her, without moving, as if to see what her reaction was.

"Arthur," Nancy said, attempting to sound serious, that he might understand there was a problem.

The moment she spoke Arthur leaped down off the stairs onto the floor, dropping forward, his front legs right out in front of him, back end sticking up, as if he were a lion about to leap.

Nancy looked at him, perplexed. "Seriously," she began to say, but before she could finish he reacted.

Arthur bounced up and then back into his position, before yapping at her, a gruff half-bark, more playful than insistent.

"No," Nancy said, doing her best to maintain a serious tone.

Arthur gruffed again, still looking intently at her, only now sliding sideways left and right, like a bull charging around for his target.

"No, I won't," Nancy said, trying hard not to smile. As annoyed as she was at the clothes on the floor, she couldn't help but find him funny.

Arthur barked louder than he had intended, before charging at the shirt. He grabbed it and turned, running back upstairs like a thief stealing away.

"Oh, no you don't," Nancy called, trying to grab the end of the shirt, but he was too fast. As she ran after him, struggling to get up the stairs with feet numb from the cold she could see more clothes on the stairs, all strewn around.

"Bad dog," Nancy called half-heartedly. The way she felt as she chased after him and the smirk on her face said two very different things about how she felt. It was annoying having to pick up after him, not to mention whether they were clean clothes or from the laundry basket, but as annoying as it was it was still a change, and perhaps fun with it. Life had its ups and downs, and at times could be mundane, but it was clear with Arthur around it would never be dull.

As Nancy finally got to the top of the stairs she immediately saw Arthur, stood half in and half out of the living room doorway, looking back at her. His mouth was open, panting away, eyes bright like twin sapphires mirroring the bright white outside. He was no longer hunched over, instead watching her to see what she did next.

"Arthur," Nancy said, her voice lower, quieter. She may well have been tired, but she still fancied a runaround with him, if that was what it took. Nancy dropped the small bag she had been carrying abruptly to the floor, at which Arthur closed his mouth, still watching her.

This time it was different, two could play games. Nancy hunched over, as if she were about to break out into a run. Arthur reacted quickly, barking at her once. He knew playtime when it was about to begin.

The moment Nancy jumped ahead to chase him, Arthur yapped, spinning around before disappearing into the living room. Off she went, to see him in there in the middle of the room. As he saw her enter Arthur quickly grabbed one of the many teddies from the floor in his mouth. It was clearly too large for him, a huge white fluffy thing, its head bouncing around like a marionette being pulled on invisible strings. He dragged it away, managing only a few feet before having to grab it again, trying to get a better hold.

Nancy struggled not to laugh. She had never had a dog of her own, a kind of regret that her parents had constantly said no to pets, not even a hamster. It was certainly different, but she knew the instincts she had about her children and what was best for them would guide her in how best to care for a dog. At least that was what she hoped.

"OK, that's enough," Nancy said, standing up straight. As much fun as it was, she was concerned about the teddy getting ripped if he got too carried away, something that Billy might not like too much. It was very early days for their new pet, and the last thing they wanted was for anyone to get upset so soon. No doubt it would happen, if she knew her children, but for now it just needed managing.

Arthur, of course, was having too much fun; as if he was going to stop. It didn't matter that the teddy bear was twice his size, there were plenty of other ones to choose from, so he dropped it. He looked straight at her, but before she could thank him for being good he ran over, grabbing another. This one was a giraffe, yellow with black spots.

Nancy's eyes lit up, seeing the pooch grab one of Billy's favorite comforters.

"No, boy, leave that," she said, which he promptly ignored. It was almost time for panic. The last thing she wanted to do was to run for him, but it might come to it. Nancy quickly unfastened her coat, dropping in onto one of the large armchairs, before slipping off her shoes.

Arthur was having none of it, running around in circles in the room, just about evading Nancy's grasp.

"No," Nancy struggled to say as she tried to leap to grab him. Each time he would wriggle free and be away. His time on the streets had taught him something worthwhile in such circumstances; how not to get caught.

Something had to be done, because otherwise it would all end in tears. Nancy stopped what she was doing, at which Arthur took her lead and stopped, watching her every move. Without saying another word she walked out, calmly and quietly, leaving him to it. It was a master stroke, as he dropped the teddy, waiting and listening to see if she might return. She didn't.

Seconds passed, without any sound. Finally curiosity got the better of him, as he walked out of the living room, looking up and down the hall, seeing no one there. Arthur's ears pricked up, as he listened for any sounds to see where she had gone.

The sound was like a hissing noise, coming from his left, his favorite place: the kitchen! Merrily he trotted off, standing just short of entering fully. He knew it was a trap; she was up to something. As he looked he saw Nancy stood in one corner, one hand on her hip, looking at him as if she had all the answers. Now he was in her domain, her lair, where she could make all the demands. There were no teddies to rescue him now.

"Hello, Arthur," Nancy said, at which he looked warily around. Was there a trap about to spring? What was going to happen?

Then it hit him. It wasn't quite the trap or surprise that had got his instincts going, not the shock that might make him run, but something much trickier, more wily, even smarter than he was.

What hit him wasn't an obvious trap, more cunning than that. It was food, hiding somewhere, only he had to find it first. Up went Arthur's head, his nose out, sniffing the air, following the scent, finding that magic.

"Oooh, what's that, boy?" Nancy asked, her eyes narrowed like a leopard waiting to grab its prey. Arthur wasn't what she was after though, it was the teddy, which she quickly snatched away, holding it tightly. Job done.

Of course, she was far too kind to mislead him, there would have to be something for him, otherwise he might not trust her next time.

Arthur continued to nose around, sniffing here and there, following the invisible trail. Whatever it was seemed delicious, too good to resist.

"Go find it, where is it?" Nancy whispered, now stood by the door.

Whatever it was smelled so good he could almost taste it, like some kind of meat, perhaps his favorite. Gently Arthur walked ahead, further into the kitchen. He leaned a little towards the table, but no, the scent died a little there. He leaned over to the cooker, realizing he was moving away again. Then the scent was strong, leading him right to it. Whatever it was seemed fine, and he hoped would taste as good.

There it was, perhaps, because all he could see was a red thing, a piece of it, sticking out on the edge of the worktop. It was too high for him, just beyond his reach, but he wasn't going to give up, not that easily.

Arthur walked over to the cupboards, looking up, sniffing still, until he was right next to it. He could jump onto his hind legs and maybe grab at it, but he knew she was there, watching. What would she do if he did jump? Would she shout, or would she shove him away? He still didn't know her well enough to be sure, and the last thing he wanted was for this lovely new family to get angry with him. Instead he waited, impatiently, looking back at her, then back to the food.

Nancy chuckled quietly to herself, not wanting to disturb the moment. She thought to say something, to egg him on, but he was doing fine by himself, so she would wait and see what he did. It was obvious he would do something, because, well, of course he would; what dog could resist fresh food?

Turning back to the counter, Arthur hopped a little from his front legs, dropping back, feeling sheepish, waiting for the call to stop which never came. It never would. The edge of it stuck out just enough so that he could see it, so close and yet so far. The torment was too much, but so far she hadn't complained, so he would have to keep going, carefully, just so that he could get what he wanted, that splendid thing, without her reacting. Now who was the clever one? He could steal it away without her knowing, and it would be gone before she had a chance to object.

The smell seemed nice, reminding him of other meat he had tasted, but he just couldn't see it.

Nancy leaned against the door frame, doing her very best not to laugh as Arthur stood up, sat down, wagged his tail, turned around in a circle and finally looked back at her. It was clear that he wouldn't do anything while she was watching, so she turned and walked out, back to *do something else*. At least that was what Arthur thought, as he too turned and once again began eyeing whatever it was that was sat on the kitchen counter.

It was too much, something had to give, so Arthur stretched, lifting himself up as much as he could without jumping. Once again he glanced back, to see no one there, and this time he jumped, fronts paws almost to the counter, his head trying to peer over it. Still, he was just too short.

Quietly, Nancy walked back, only now leaning her head around the frame, looking in just enough to see, and quietly enough that she wouldn't disturb him. There he was, stood up leaning against the worktop, trying to see over. The food was a tiny distance away, so close. Arthur pushed himself up further, as if he were up on the claws of his hind legs. He stretched his neck, just inching slightly higher, pressing against the hard worktop, desperate to taste those goodies. Nearly there, not quite.

"What's going on?" a voice asked behind Nancy, making her jump so much she almost screamed. She barely held on, turning to see Abigail stood, having returned from school, her bag dragging on the hall carpet.

"Shhhh," Nancy insisted, finger to her mouth, smiling. Abigail quietly looked around her mother, to see Arthur, as if he were trying to pole vault over something, only without the pole.

Abigail looked at Nancy, her brow furrowed, wondering what on earth was going on. Nancy gesticulated, but didn't want to speak to spoil the moment.

Just a tiny bit more, Arthur thought. So there it was, and out went the tongue, licking the air around it, trying to grasp the piece of meat, sat there alone on the cupboards, as if it were calling to him and meant the difference between life and death.

"Why don't you just give it to him?" Abigail whispered, loud enough for him to hear, but it didn't matter, because nothing would stop him.

Just as Nancy was about to give in, Arthur finally nudged the meat with his tongue, lapping at it, until it moved, slowly, slightly, then again, until he shifted enough for him to take a hold. There, finally, like a wolf trying to catch a sheep, he grabbed at it with his mouth, pulling it until it fell on the floor. It was a thick piece of meat, cooked but fresh enough.

"Arthur," a voice called loudly, suddenly making him step back. His eyes never wavered, though he recognized the voice, that of Billy as he entered. As loving as he was, and as friendly as he clearly was being, Arthur was still wary enough of people to think twice before doing anything that he knew might be wrong.

"Oh," Nancy said, intending to say her son had ruined the moment, but stopping herself, realizing it wasn't his fault, he wouldn't know, and could hardly be admonished for doing so.

"Well done, bozo," Abigail said, not quite feeling the same level of restraint of her mother when it came to dealing with her brother.

"Go on, boy, eat it," Billy said quickly, without a moment's hesitation. Arthur might well have still thought twice over what to do, in any other circumstances, but given it was food, and wonderful food at that, he just went for it, quickly grabbing it and chewing it up. If anyone complained now he would just ignore them, playing dumb. He was never the type of dog who might growl or bark if anyone got close to him while eating, but he sure would fight for his grub if need be. Playfully, anyway.

"Are we at that stage where we watch dogs eat then?" another voice asked, at which they all turned to look. All except Arthur that was, who had finished his meat and was licking the floor as if it too might taste the same.

"Oh hello, love," Nancy said, looking at Stan with a smile. Stan leaned in and pecked her on the cheek, at which Abigail screwed up her face, pronouncing an obvious yuck, before walking away.

"Look, Dad, Arthur has just eaten half a cow," Billy said, giggling to himself.

"Oh nice," Stan replied. "Makes a change from eating half a chicken."

"No, that was Abigail did that," Billy shouted, laughing.

"I think Arthur could do with a run later," Stan said. He was stood looking tired, as if he had all the worry of the world on his shoulders. As he looked it seemed as if he weren't looking at anything, removing his coat but not thinking where he might put it.

"Here, I'll take that," Nancy said, aware why he was tired. She knew where he had been, and that it had been a long day for him.

"Where is he gonna run, Dad, up and down the stairs?" Billy asked cheerfully.

Stan smiled back as best he could. "On the park, over the road maybe."

"Yeah," Billy called, sounding too excited for his own good. "Can we go now?"

"No, you have to get changed out of your school clothes, and you also need to have your tea first," Nancy insisted.

"What's for tea, Mum?" Billy asked.

"Nothing, the dog just ate it," Nancy said, looking seriously at him. The smile on Billy's face instantly disappeared, as if for a moment he really believed it.

Stan laughed briefly. He was tired. It had been a long day, but he was thankful his life was all about his family now, and he knew he could always rely on his children and his wife to keep him going. Nothing would change that.

CHAPTER NINE

"Right, come on then, let's get him out," Stan said suddenly, making them all jump. The house was warm with the central heating on. It was so cozy even Arthur didn't imagine going out, curled up at the feet of the man who appeared to show him the least amount of affection. Billy looked at him, wondering why he did so, instead of being with him, the one who provided the most fun.

Nobody moved. Even Arthur kept his head down on the carpet, hoping that whatever was intended he wasn't a part of it. Still, deep down he knew he needed to go, and the word outside was one he was fully aware of. His mind said no, his body said yes.

"I have homework," Abigail said politely, as she tapped away on the television remote control looking for music videos.

"Looks like it," Nancy said, eying her across her newspaper.

"Oh, so you're coming with us then?" Stan asked, looking directly at his wife.

"Of course," Nancy said, surprising Stan.

"Well done, Mum," Billy said, smiling at her.

"Of course not," Nancy said, chuckling to herself. "Far too cold out here for me."

Stan looked at Billy. He knew he didn't even need to ask his son if he was going. Clearly he was. If Billy had been a bit older he would gladly have let him walk Arthur alone on the park, but it was across a busy main road and the light was failing.

"Why did we get a dog again, someone remind me?" Stan asked, only half intending his question to be serious.

"Ohhh," Billy said, so surprised that anyone could even think such a thing, let alone say it.

"Stan," Nancy said, in such a way the her displeasure over it was clear.

53

Abigail remained silent. For some reason she struggled with, even she found it wrong, but that was at odds with her stance of not caring at all, about anything, so she decided not to voice her confusion.

"I'm just kidding," Stan said quickly. As much as he was willing to go along with the wishes of the family, deep down his feelings didn't quite mirror theirs. However he felt, he had no idea why he might even be a little reluctant, but he was.

"Right," Stan said, standing up quickly. He would dwell on it no longer, as he strode out into the hall.

Billy jumped up, following suit, at which Arthur felt unable to resist the urge to do the same. He had an idea of what was coming, but he had learned to understand that nothing could be taken for granted, not in his life.

They were a procession, walking in a trio, along the hallways, down the stairs as Stan flicked light switches on, lighting everywhere up.

Out of the window they could see the sun had begun to dip quickly behind the horizon, leaving a reddish hue to the sky. The skies were no longer filled with flecks of snow, but the ground outside was still a winter wonderland.

"Can we build a snowman?" Billy asked as he quickly pulled on his coat.

"It'll probably be too cold, I doubt the snow will stick together," Stan replied, as he wrapped himself tightly in a scarf, gloves and coat. It was the last thing he wanted to be doing on such an evening, but at least for him it might help clear his head.

"Great, I can't wait," Billy said excitedly, as his father's words were purely an agreement for what he wanted.

Arthur stood looking at them both as they prepared to go out. He knew all too well what it meant, but in part he loved it. In the time before, he would happily go out in all weathers, because after the fun they would go back and dry off, get warm, and perhaps if he was lucky, there would be a snack. Now he knew it wasn't always like that, he had learned that life didn't always offer guarantees.

"Come on, boy, put your lead on," Billy said as he lifted the chain from the coat hook. Arthur paced around, excited to get out. He had been so comfortable he hadn't thought about his needs, but now it was like a dam waiting to burst.

Stan opened the door and stepped out, feeling a rush of bitterly cold air sweeping in.

Arthur went to charge out, only to notice the abject cold, as Stan's feet crunched on the ice cold snow outside. He stopped dead, turning slightly to see Billy behind him.

"Let's go," Billy said, worrying for his new dog and how he might be feeling. "You're alright, I'm here for you, I won't let you go."

The words struck home for Stan; the thought that it wasn't temporary, that things had changed. He acknowledged to himself mentally that he had imagined it short term, that the change in their lives brought on by Arthur wouldn't last, and once again he would go again. He felt sick at the thought of it, and ashamed at the feeling he dared to have.

"Out you go," Billy insisted to Arthur, but he was having none of it. Billy laughed a little, looking to his dad for signs of what to do, but it was clear his mind was elsewhere, lost in thought.

Billy nudged at Arthur, but again he just looked back then out, remaining in the doorway. His body was telling him to go out, he needed to do his business, but his mind was telling him it was cold out, and he might not get back in.

"Gooooo," Billy said, now leaning over to push him. Arthur resisted more, at which Billy kneeled down, leaning right behind him, placing both his hands on his bottom.

"Billy, what are you doing?" Stan asked, stood watching them both while wishing he too was indoors.

"He won't move," Billy said, pushing with all his might. As much as he tried, Arthur was having none of it, pushing back as well as he could.

With all his tiny might Billy leaned into Arthur, pressing against him, struggling to grip on the lower hall floor, as Arthur twisted and turned, seeking to avoid having to out into the winter night. In his mind he thought the moment he was out he might never get back in, and no more food, no more warmth, and perhaps no more love.

As foolish as it was, Billy laughed joyously, loving every moment of their hijinks. For Arthur, well he found it more than a little embarrassing, as a little boy shoved him this way and that, rolling around all over, trying to shove the pooch out where he needed to be.

Finally, his patience wearing thin, Stan walked back, connected the lead, and tugged gently on Arthur's collar. Billy watched his father as he pulled, so that he too would push, and together they would make sure Arthur was out.

That was the plan anyway, but they had no idea how stubborn Arthur could be. Stan pulled, enough he thought so as to make a difference, but not too much that it might hurt him. Billy pushed, so much that he slipped sideways and rolled out of the doorway, onto the cold snow outside. Shivering with its bitterness, Billy wasn't bothered, he was too busy giggling away as if it were the funniest thing he had ever seen. He was wrapped up on the innocence of youth, at that moment in time where the only things in life that mattered were the things he could see in front of him. Right now, then and there, all he could see was a large dog's bottom, and the funny look that dog kept giving him, all teeth and wide eyes.

Even Stan found himself chuckling, trying not to, because he wanted to get out and done and back, but as stern as he tried to be, his son's behavior was infectious, that silly oddness where it didn't matter who was looking, the mirth of the moment roaming around them. Nobody thought about it then, but in years to come they would look back on it and remember, and each time they would think of Arthur, and laugh.

"Come on, Arthur," Stan pleaded. "Time for walkies." That was it, the magic word, the thing that changed everything. Arthur suddenly stopped fighting, instead standing up straight, tail wagging as if he had just discovered for the first time what a good boy he was. His eyes lit up, ears right out, looking directly at Stan. Had he said it? Had he said what he thought he had?

"Yes, that's it, come on," Stan said, at which Arthur's ears dropped again. That wasn't it.

"Walkies," Billy said, at which Arthur turned sharply, looking directly at him as if he were made of dog snacks. Once again his tail wagged, excitement coursing through him.

"Right, I see," Stan said, finally getting it.

Billy stood up, dusting the frozen snow from his trousers and coat. "Let's go walkies, Arthur," he said as he ran outside.

"Who's a good boy then?" Stan said, only wanting to encourage him more. He slowed, looking up at Stan as if he understood every word he had said. It was another unexpected call to him, listening to the voice and those words, which sounded so familiar. A memory occurred to him of another time, with another person, who was so full of love. Every time she would say those things, and off they went together, enjoying so much fun and love. What he would give to have that again.

The thought was washed away as Billy threw a small snowball at Arthur, missing him completely, instead hitting Stan on the side. It didn't matter, because Billy laughed anyway.

"OK, let's save that for the park," Stan said, looking forward to it.

"Can I take my sledge?" Billy asked, breathless before it had even begun.

"Not tonight, it's getting a bit late. Maybe at the weekend, we can all go for a walk in the snow," Stan replied. It sounded like it would be fun, but it would have to wait.

Billy didn't even wait for his response, instead he was off to the gate and out, to the driveway, slapping his hands together while calling for Arthur.

Arthur for his part jumped and pranced around, chomping at the bit to go for a run.

It was all too much excitement, so Stan broke out into a run, as best he could in the conditions. "Right, Billy, stop at the traffic lights, wait til it goes green, wait for me," Stan insisted as he was dragged along by Arthur.

Light had faded and given way to a surround of sodium orange lighting. It affected the look of the snow, as car tracks crisscrossed the road with splashes of wet slush. As night had fallen the slush was beginning to turn to thick ice, masked by an air of white vapor.

"We won't stay out long," Stan said as the three of them made their way to the park.

The wide expanse of the park was covered in broken snow, trodden by a thousand and more footsteps, but still it was beautiful. Trees that adorned the park were coated in a thick roof of white, and even bushes and plants, shorn of their leaves, looked depressed from the weight of the snowfall. The lights around the park were different, a brighter white so safer in the surrounding darkness.

As Stan and Billy walked across the crunching snow, Arthur leaped and bounded, doing his best to run free, aware of the lead. It was all Stan could do to keep him in check while still allowing him to look around.

Arthur stopped near a bench, sniffing for all his worth, peering this way and that, as if he were on the trail of something important.

Billy laughed. "What's he doing, Dad?" he asked.

"He'll be sniffing for other dogs," Stan replied, thankful for a moment's respite from the pulling.

"Really? So he can smell dogs that have walked around here?"

"Yes, well, he can sniff something from them," Stan answered, trying to look away, obviously not wanting to discuss it much more. He was surprised how little his own son understood about dogs. He wouldn't admit it, but it also proved why it was good they had Arthur, so that his children could finally understand what pets and animals were about.

"Sniff what?" Billy asked, immediately realizing what it was they might pick up on.

"Well," Stan began to say.

"Oh," Billy said, looking at his father, but not wanting to. "Can we let him off, to run around?" he asked, quickly before anything more was said.

"Yes, er, I mean, no," Stan spluttered. "If we let him off now he might run and we might not get him back on his lead again."

"Oh," Billy said again. "Can I hold his lead then?" he asked, looking at his father is if being denied might be the worst thing in the world to him.

"I guess so. You have to hold him tight and don't let him go, no matter what, OK?" Stan replied.

Billy nodded, making sure he did so enough that his father would be very well aware of just how important it was to him.

All the while Arthur had been lost in his own little world, oblivious to the others. There wasn't much to sniff at, given the frosty conditions, but he would do his best. Still, it was all well and good, but nothing compared to a good run. If anyone said so, he would be off like a shot, that much was certain in his mind.

Slowly Stan handed the handle for the lead over to Billy. It was a leather strap, attached to a solid chain lead. He lifted it over his son's hand, to his wrist, wrapping it carefully across.

"Now, hold that bit tightly, and then walk him, see how he goes," Stan said, stepping carefully back, as if he had just lit the touch paper on a firework.

"Yeah," Billy said excitedly, just as Arthur had cocked his leg on a nearby bush. Straight after he began to scrape the snow, wiping it away harshly.

"What's he doing now?" Billy asked, doing his best not to get splashed by the flash of brittle snow.

"He's covering up, because he's a good boy," Stan said, realizing he was miming someone else, someone he had rarely thought about until recently. He wanted to berate himself mentally, but wasn't sure what for.

"Oh," Billy said once again, aware that he was repeating himself. "I bet he'd like to run," he said, looking at his father, but he was clearly distracted.

"Sorry, what did you say, he wants what?" Stan asked, still not properly listening.

"Run, he wants to run," Billy shouted, at which Arthur did just that, as he had been ordered to. Arthur ran all of a sudden, leaping away, more out of instinct than desire to be away.

"Oh," Stan said, now his turn to be shocked, as Arthur ran so strongly he took Billy with him, knocking him off his feet and dragging him across the snow.

"Dad," Billy shouted.

"Billy," Stan shouted.

Arthur just ran, enjoying every moment of it, dragging Billy along as if it was meant to be. Clearly it was part of the fun.

Suddenly Stan realized what he should be doing, breaking out into a run after them.

"Stop," Stan shouted, struggling to stay upright in the slippery snow.

Billy tried his best to grab the lead with his other hand, but was too busy flailing around.

Arthur carried on, wound up even more by all the shouting. He was so pleased that they were enjoying it too, and even better, the little boy was running with him. Sort of.

A pleasant and unexpected smell caught his attention, making him stop dead. That was it, as he sniffed around, Billy struggled to stand up. Stan came upon them, quickly grasping hold of his son.

"Wow," Billy said, pushing the loop of the lead's handle from his wrist.

"No, let me," Stan said, trying to take hold of it.

"All I said was run and," Billy began to say.

Arthur once again leaped away, only now the lead was gone, no longer attached to anyone.

"Billy," Stan shouted instinctively while still looking at Arthur. Billy looked at Stan, wondering why he was calling Arthur by his name.

"Ohhh," Stan called, trying to run again. He had come outside still wearing ordinary shoes, only now to realize what a mistake he had made.

"Arthur," Billy whispered as he finally understood what the problem was. He ran, following his father, trudging through the snow, trying not to allow himself to get upset as he watched Arthur sprint away across the park.

"Arthur, stop," Stan finally shouted. At first Arthur seemed to slow a little, before once again sprinting away. Stan continued to run as best he could, trying not to slip in the increasingly icy conditions. All snowfall had stopped, and now as the skies cleared and stars provided illumination, bitterly cold air descended, hardening everything around them.

At the edge of the park Arthur seemed to stop as white plumes of breath puffed from his mouth. It had been a while since he had run anywhere properly, but it felt good. Even so, Arthur could feel how cold it was becoming. It would be the coldest night of the year.

"Here, boy," Billy cried, doing his best to keep up. Tears rolled down his icy cheeks, as fears washed over him that their new dog would leave them forever.

"Arthur," Stan called again, as he once more determined to run for him. Just as he was about to round a large bush, believing he was in sight of coming to him, he heard a loud snap, followed by a cry behind him.

It was an impossible choice, at first, to get their dog, to stop him running away again, or to go back for his son. Of course, there was no choice, but it didn't matter which he went with, because either way there would be tears. Stan slowed, turned to look at his son, laying on the floor, moving slowly. Arthur rounded a corner and disappeared, gone from sight, seemingly gone from their lives.

"Dad," Billy cried. Stan felt like crying himself, but he wouldn't, because he wasn't allowed to. He had to be the strong one, the shoulder for others to cry on.

"Alright, son, I'm coming," Stan called, shuffling back to Billy.

"I fell," Billy said, trying to sit up, crying.

"Are you hurt?" Stan asked, collecting his son gently, afraid to move him in case he was badly injured.

"My leg hurts. I fell over that branch," Billy said, pointing to an area where children had been playing.

"You're OK, though?" Stan asked, hopefully.

"I'm alright, but where's Arthur?" Billy asked, struggling to speak and control his sadness.

"He's gone, love. He just ran off."

Billy cried more, more than he could ever remember. Stan picked him up, cradling him in his arms.

"Come on, let's go home," Stan said, pulling Billy closer to him.

Off they went, walking back across the park, across the beautiful white snow, back towards their home which seemed just a little bit darker now.

CHAPTER TEN

It was late, much later than it should have been. It was the beginning of a school night, and Billy should have been in bed much sooner. It was difficult rushing, because whatever choice was made, it wouldn't be good for any of them.

Stan had lowered Billy to the ground once he had stop crying long enough. All he had done was walk slowly, head down, lost in his own misery. It was obvious what had to be done, but he was tired, and simply didn't think he had the strength. It had been a long day, one of the longest of his life, full of unspoken regrets, and now this. Sometimes life doesn't give us a choice, if we want to be good parents.

"I tell you what, let's get you home and into bed, and then I will go look for him," Stan said, feeling all the more weary for having offered, but still knowing he had to do it.

Billy looked up at him, a spark of hope in his eye. "Really, you think you can find him?" he asked, looked so different for that semblance of hope.

Stan shrugged his shoulders. He knew better from experience than to make promises he couldn't keep, but neither could he let his son down. He couldn't live with the thought that his son might not think he was that amazing.

"I can only go look," Stan said as they once again crossed the slushy road.

"Stay out all night, til you find him," Billy said, clearly believing he would. Stan gently nudged him with his hand behind his back, before placing it on his shoulder as they walked. Across they went, over the slushy road, back towards their house, up the driveway.

"I'll tell Mum you've lost him," Billy said, his voice so weak he feared he might break out crying again.

Stan looked at him in surprise, as if he were to blame, but of course arguing would only make it worse.

Everywhere seemed dark, as if they were out on a midnight walk, even though it was barely towards seven o'clock.

"Alright, son," Stan said, struggling himself for how to handle it. He had thought that he might feel some sense of relief that he might not have to contend with a dog, let alone a dog belonging to his mother, but deep down it was far different for him.

As they approached the gate, light spilled out onto the garden. The door was part open, and stood in the doorway was Nancy, looking as cold as they felt.

"Mum," was all Billy could say, his voice betrayed by sadness, as once again tears rolled down his cheeks.

"What's up, love, are you cold?" she asked.

"No, it's," Billy tried to say, unable to give life to the words.

"It's Arthur," Stan said for him, determined to go look for him.

"Oh, yes, Arthur. Foolish dog," Nancy said as she folded her arms, clearly feeling the biting cold. She had changed into a dressing gown and slippers after taking a shower, and stood outside she clearly had regretted the decision.

Billy stopped, looking at his mother, unable to think what to do.

"Yes, I have no idea what goes through that dog's mind," Nancy said. "I was just coming out of the shower and heard that banging, and then I opened the door to see him sat right outside. I've no idea why," Nancy said, unaware of the situation.

Arthur was sat in the corner of the garden, between the house and the shed.

"Oh, oh boy," Billy cried, running over to him. He fell to his knees, wrapping his arms around him. Even Arthur was surprised, having no clue what the fuss was all about. To him, all he could think of was that it was cold, and he wanted to be inside again. He had a chance, to run back to his home, and show them how much he wanted to be there. He even showed it, with a jump and a thud at the door.

"I guess that saves me going looking for him," Stan said.

"Really. So how did he end up here knocking at the door to get in?" Nancy asked.

"I'll explain in a bit. Let's all get in and get warm," Stan said as he watched Billy hug Arthur, who offered his best, most innocent look.

Billy stood up and walked towards the open door. He remained half turned between the door and Arthur, looking back and forth, arms out.

"Come on, let's go in," Billy said, more a plea full of hope than a demand. Arthur didn't need any further encouragement, rushing past them all and through the door. He barely stopped to look to see who was there and what was in his way, before rushing up the stairs and away.

"I guess he wanted to be in," Stan said, as if he were impressing something upon himself.

"Come on, cheeky boy, time you were in bed," Nancy said as she welcomed Billy in. She took off his coat and boots and hugged him. "Why are you so upset?"

Rubbing his eyes, Billy looked at her as best he could, but struggled to keep his eyes open. As he was about to speak he leaned his head back and yawned deeply.

"Oh right, it's like that, is it?" Nancy asked, standing up beside him. She placed both hands under his arms and lifted him, hugging him to her.

"Bed time," Stan said as he walked in, closing the door. He thought about making a joke about it being his own bed time, but figured no one would find it funny, even if he wouldn't mind an early night.

The three went up the stairs, with Nancy doing her best to carry Billy. Stan thought to offer to carry him, but knew she wanted to do it. Maternal instincts and all.

As they made their way along the hall towards the living room, Abigail walked out. "Hey, why is it I don't get carried to bed like that?" she asked.

Stan didn't wait, walking quickly past Nancy, he headed straight to her. Abigail watched him in horror as he approached, realizing she had said the wrong thing.

"OK, bed time, Abigail, I shall carry you," Stan said, arms out ready to scoop her up.

"No," Abigail shouted, running into the living room. As Stan followed her, Arthur shot out from behind the door, barking for all he was worth. Stan jumped back, withdrawing, surprised by his actions.

"Yeah, you tell him, Arthur," Abigail called, laughing at his behavior.

"Arthur," Nancy said, growing tired from carrying Billy.

One word from her was enough, so he stopped, looking at her as if she had shouted at the top of her voice at him.

"I guess he knows who's in charge," Abigail said, smirking at her father.

"I guess so," Stan replied. Abigail looked at him, smiling, finding it all so funny.

"Don't you have some homework to do?" Nancy asked. She didn't wait for her daughter to answer, instead turning to make her way to take Billy to bed.

Abigail remained silent at the horrifying suggestion. Homework indeed, as if that ever happened. She didn't respond, but remained fully aware of her father's grinning at her. Payback.

"Mum," Billy said, surprising his mother. She had thought he was so shattered he was asleep already.

"Yes, love," Nancy replied softly.

"Can Arthur sleep with me tonight?" he asked, rubbing his eyes again.

Nancy stopped and turned, to see Stan at the living room doorway, looking back. "I think Arthur needs his own bed now," he said, smiling.

"OK, Dad," Billy said, once again resting his head on her shoulder.

"Right, let's get you into your pajamas and into bed," Nancy said, making her way up the stairs.

Stan walked out into the hall, opening a tall cupboard door, before leaning in and rummaging around through the many things inside. Eventually he pulled out a large knitted blanket, before closing the door. As he did he got a fright to see Abigail stood right in front of him.

"Wow, you're really into this dog thing then," she said, at which Stan looked at Arthur. There he was again, as always, looking at him, tail wagging more and more whenever their eyes met.

"Well," Stan began to say, but hesitated. "He needs his own bed."

"Great, hear that, Arthur? You have your own bed," Abigail said, looking at him sat nearby. The look on his face was a picture of happiness, ears up, eyes sparkling in the room's bright lights, occasionally turning his head side to side as if he were mock confused.

"Shall I put it in here, maybe near the radiator?" Abigail asked, hands out ready to receive the large blanket. The look on her face wasn't expectant, she knew something wasn't right, she could read her dad like a book, and things weren't quite so perfect. What she didn't know was why.

"It's fine, I shall put it in place, and make sure he knows he has to sleep there," Stan said.

"Surely if you put it down and point to it and say bed, he will go there and lay down?" Abigail asked, a perfectly reasonable question.

"Er, yes, but," Stan tried to say. Abigail watched him, well aware that she might only say so much before he would walk away.

"Yes then?" she asked, at which he did indeed turn and walk away. He saw no reason to discuss it further, his perfectly reasonable plans to ensure Arthur was safe and happy, in his own little place.

"Arthur," Stan called, from the safety of the hall as he walked away, quickly before his awkward daughter could ask any more difficult questions. Arthur didn't need any further encouragement, quickly running out into the hall.

"Come on," Stan said, no longer bothering to look at him. He knew he was being followed as he listened to the small patter of paws behind him. Down the stairs they went, quietly into the darkness. Stan didn't bother to switch on the lights, he knew the place well enough not to need to.

The only illumination came through glass panels in the doorway, lit up by the bright white snow outside. Slow ice flakes had once again begun to drift down, covering the garden outside and with it burying any signs of their being out there. The walk, the running, the tears, it was all blanketed in a soft mesh of white lace until all that remained were bumps suggesting something happened, but it no longer mattered.

Stan walked to the end of the hallway. The flooring had no carpeting, as it wasn't needed. There were no places to sit or remain, only for storage, and several doors, one of which went to the boiler that Arthur knew all too well. The best thing about it was that it was warm in there, but the worst thing was that it was almost too dark to see, and of course the door would close and there he might remain. He had no interest in going back.

As Stan walked along Arthur slowed, mindful of the possible intent, perhaps to take him outside, or into the boiler room. Neither offered anything for him.

"Come on, over here. It's nice and warm here," Stan said, as he placed the blanket down onto the hard floor.

Arthur stared at him, still with his ears high, still trusting that he would do the right thing. The floor felt cold under the pads of his paws, but it was still far better than anything else he had experienced while on the streets. He thought of the night in the derelict building nearby, circled up, shivering in the cold. Nothing could compare to the comfort and safety of being under the bed, but a blanket on the floor was still good.

Kneeling down, Stan looked once more at Arthur. He felt torn, wanting to get it done with and go back upstairs, but he also felt a twinge of guilt, that he might not be offering what was his mother's dog as much care and attention as he should. Still, in his mind it wasn't all his own fault. To him, she bore some of the blame for how things had ended up, if only she had done more of what he wanted when she was around, then perhaps he would have been happier. As if he were always right.

Finally Arthur made his way onto the oblong shape that the blanket represented. Stan stood up, backing away a little, looking at him, hopefully. After a few seconds Arthur turned around once, then again, then scratched at it, as if trying to tuft it up. Stan smiled to himself, impressed that the dog knew what it was for. There was no need to click his fingers, no instruction to stay, no need for orders. He thought to commend him, perhaps to pat him on the head, but then he might take it as a sign to leave with him, so instead turned and walked away.

Arthur was no fool, as the moment Stan began to walk away he looked at him, watching his movements. The moment Stan got to the stairs he turned around to look, just one last time, to make sure he wasn't being followed. He wasn't, because Arthur was sat, in the middle of the blanket, looking at him, as if with one word he might break out into a run and go for cuddles and a hug. It never came, no fuss, no interest, simply a look and then Stan turned and was gone, back up the stairs.

It was an odd end to a very unusual day, for both of them. Stan was thankful, allowed to go back upstairs, get ready for bed, and to sleep in peace. It was good that he could rest knowing Arthur would be on his bed, down the stairs, in the hall. Arthur, of course, well, he had others ideas.

CHAPTER ELEVEN

It didn't take too long. He waited long enough to make sure no one caught him, and no one made him go back again. Arthur could naturally tell when the house was settled, because movement eventually ceased, lights filtering from up the stairs disappeared, and any and all sounds stopped. The house fell silent, and slowly but surely cold air began to pervade all around him. The heating was off, at least close to him, and he was surrounded by only darkness.

For a younger dog this might well be overwhelming, and perhaps they might choose to call out, for their mother, or for the presence of someone else, hopefully one to love them. Arthur was older, wiser, a little smarter about things, but he thought and felt as much as any dog, and likely as much as any person too.

The first shiver he had was a sign for him to move. He did so, lifting his front paws until he remained sat, looking out into the night. He could just about make out the hallway, the doors beside, and what little light there was outside from the snow filtering in. Then, while stood up, he shivered again. He thought to walk round in a circle and lay again, in a tightly wound ball, but this was Arthur, so unlike other dogs. He wouldn't just sit there and take it, and neither would he howl, or demand attention. Instead, he would go wandering, and see something of the place. After all, it was his home too.

As dark as it was, he still had fine vision, and could make out where he was going. There would be no problems at all, so he thought, until he walked unto a broomstick leaning against the wall nearby. He knew what it would do, but even so when the stick hit the floor the loud crack still made him jump. He stopped dead, waiting, looking at the stairs, waiting for someone to come down, calling out, complaining about the noise, but no one came. He was lucky, because two floors up, no one could hear such a thing.

Once again Arthur padded ahead, slower and more cautious. He stopped at the outside door, looking through the clear glass. The corners were smeared from frost as snow continued to fall, light enough so that it wouldn't become impossible to move outside, but heavy enough to cover everything so that it seemed like the land outside was reborn while everyone slept.

Arthur didn't need to be outside to understand how it might feel to be out there, he didn't even want to think about it. The only use a place like that had was to do his business, and for now that could wait.

So once again off he went, slowly walking up the stairs. There were no lights, but that didn't mean there wasn't still someone there. He could picture getting to the top of the stairs in his mind, only to see the big man there, stood, arms crossed, tapping his foot, staring at him, barking at him, in a way that only meant go back down. Of course, there was no one there. He was alone.

It was an opportunity, as much then as it had presented to him when he had first sneaked in. What could he do? What could he get? The possibilities were endless.

He stood in the hall, at the top of the stairs. Right down at the end was the kitchen, but before then was the living room. Slowly, ever so slowly he walked ahead, eyes wide open, until he stopped halfway down, sniffing the air. He sniffed and sniffed, as if he were trying to breathe in all the air in the house. If Billy were able to watch him he would be laughing his head off, at how funny he was, but of course he was in bed, fast asleep.

Once again Arthur walked, turning into the living room to see bright light flooding in through the huge windows. It was like a waterfall of color, casting across the room, as if it were a giant lumbering across everything, lazing there, at ease with the night.

He stopped in the middle of the floor, fully aware of how soft the carpet was underneath, compared to his blanket. It would be tempting to simply flop down there and sleep, but then it wasn't in his instincts to do so, because he was sadly so very well aware that someone might walk in on him and then the shouting would begin. That couldn't happen, no amount of hiding would protect him from shouting in that house.

The sofa and chairs looked inviting, like huge soft things wanting to be bounced on. It would be foolish to even think of going on there, because someone wouldn't like it. Arthur was a sensible dog, well trained, not inclined to do the wrong thing. Or so he thought, until he ran and jumped like a gazelle onto the large armchair in the corner. As he landed on it he bounced, like a child on a bouncy castle. He looked one way, then the other, as if he were a lion surveying his kingdom.

It was perfect, also just too inviting, so comfortable and soft, so he dropped down, still looking up proudly, as if he were on display. The chair cradled him, soaking into his shape, supporting every part of him, like a mother with a baby. This would be a fitting place to sleep, where he could lay down, roll onto his back, and snore the night away.

No, Arthur wouldn't do it, he wouldn't stay there, he couldn't, so again up he jumped, springing right over, onto the sofa. It was the same quilted softness, only longer, like a stretched out bed, one that insisted he did just that. So he did. It was fine to pull ones muscles, shaking legs, arching the back, and then dropping down, elongated, onto the sofa. For a moment he rested his head, then flopped sideways, like a chocolate log rolling down an icing hill. Then up he went, onto his back, shifting around like an itchy bear trying to catch that annoyance.

Just a few minutes, no more. He would close his eyes and rest, slumbering in perfection.

A click brought him to his senses, as a tiny fraction of light broke into the midnight black. It wasn't close, but he could hear walking, someone moving around. Arthur lifted his head, feeling so naughty, but it was difficult to resist.

Moving like a sloth, Arthur slithered off the sofa, as if his movements might bring unwanted attention down on him. He gently moved onto the carpet, like a fish out of water, wading across the floor, enjoying the sensation of softness against his belly. Quite naturally, without thinking, he began to lick the air, his tongue flailing around, slapping his mouth this way and that. He crawled further ahead, as the gentle carpet scraped his skin underneath. Who needed someone to scratch their belly when they could scramble across the floor like this and have a hundred scratches all at once?

He watched the doorway, waiting for the tall man to come in, to give him that look, the flick of the light and then point to where he knew to go, but didn't want to. He waited, and waited, and then the light upstairs went off, and a bed creaked, and once again the night fell silent. Once again, he was alone.

Even though he had been indoors and in a safe place for a while, it was still difficult to get accustomed to the silence. It felt like a huge weight sitting on his shoulders, as if the air around him had been removed and he couldn't move. In a way he was torn, partly enjoying the freedom of being outside, but loving the sense of safety of being indoors. Then there was the nature of the family, and being a part of it. Would he even like being properly alone again?

Arthur stood and walked over to the large window and sat again. The skies had cleared as the snowfall ceased, leaving an elemental nature to the skies, part dark blue, part white wisps of cloud, with flittering stars occasionally obvious in the window of the world. He opened his mouth and yawned, so much that he almost fell over. He was at peace, settled in his choice, for now, of where to be, and being happy with it. As he looked out he could see the whiteness of the ground, the myriad of different mounds of snow and ice, the frosted naked trees and the darkened houses. Freedom clearly had a price, one that involved shivering and being lonely. As joyful as it might well be being able to run anywhere and do as he pleased, it was difficult to make a sensible case for anything other than warmth, a full belly, and being loved.

As much as he felt the need to curl up and go to sleep, there was just one more thing he needed to do. Arthur stood and turned, looking into the living room. It was brighter now as the skies had cleared, allowing a roving moon to cast its glow into the room. Shadows moved gently as he looked around, as if other playthings wanted him to join in. That was it, the invitation he needed, as he dropped front legs to the floor, looking like a predator about to spring for its prey. His eyes scanned the scene, waiting for the tiniest sign to attack.

The boiler kicked in, lighting up to ensure heat spread around the home whenever it became too cold, but to Arthur it was the go signal, at which he jumped up and ahead, scrambling around the room. In one corner sat a small teddy, purple in color with long fluffy ears. It was instantly the enemy, as Arthur grabbed it and ran, dropped it then grabbed it again. It was like an explosive to him, not so much ready to go bang as to go whimper as it squeaked at him for mercy. The sudden squeak made him jump, catching him completely by surprise. He dropped the toy, looking at it as if it were somehow alive and ready to defend itself. Quickly he glanced around to see if anyone was with him, backup, that they might reassure him he was going to be alright, but no, no one there. He stepped back a bit, gave it a slight woof while trying to stare it down, and then sniffed twice. The fun was over, it was clearly far too dangerous.

Arthur snorted, breathed out and walked away. It didn't matter how hard the toy squeaked, he had won and that was that. Besides, it was time for sleep, because morning no doubt they would get him up, and keep him busy, right up until the moment when, well, when he went back to sleep again, of course.

First up were preparations, because a dog couldn't just flop down anywhere and sleep. Well, he could, but there were niceties to observe. He wandered out into the hall, made sure it was clear before going into the kitchen. The intent was to lap some nice clean water, if no pond water was available, which of course being in such a nice house it wasn't. Even the best of places had their drawbacks.

Never a moment might pass when Arthur would be stood without an odd thought dedicated to what there might be to eat, and being in a kitchen he was surrounded by temptation. There was the big metal box, sealed to ensure he couldn't get access to it, and the large wooden boxes on the wall, some with food, which were too high for him to get at, and then there was the counter, which he could just about reach, but even then he would be struggling and there might not be anything. Arthur was such a sly pooch, he could usually find a way, but for the moment he just wanted to sleep. He drank quickly at the bowl and walked off, along the hall to the stairs. He looked down, remembering the blanket, thinking what an awful thing it would be, having to sleep down there, in such an empty place, devoid of life and love. It was like the brick shelter he had slept in, the dog cage, the barn, all the places he had been put, out of sight, out of mind.

He had choices, but in reality, only one choice. He would be a good dog, and do the right thing, because he knew when it came down to it, the house only ever had one person in charge.

CHAPTER TWELVE

The alarm wasn't loud, but it was enough to do the trick. Stan was already partially awake and an eye open for it, because he was so used to his routine. Gone were the days of *oh just a few more minutes*, replaced by *I have a family now*, so duty, care and obligation called. So over he turned, nudged Nancy, at which she opened her eyes, looking at him. Nothing need be said, simply that it was a work day, and they would need to get to it, as always, because the things it brought them made it all worthwhile.

Even though he was awake first, it was Nancy who got up before him, jumping out of bed as if she were excited about something.

"Right, you seem happy. What's up with you?" Stan grumbled, rubbing his eyes to clear the sleep.

"Nothing, just things seem good, and I'm happy with how everything is," Nancy replied as she walked around the bed. Leaning over him she kissed him on the cheek. Stan smiled.

Nancy placed her dressing gown around her shoulders and buttoned it up. "Come on then, another day, another," she began.

"Another incessant day of work in order to feed the family, now including the dog," Stan replied wryly.

"Oh, very nice, mister grumpy. I guess you didn't so much get out of the wrong side of the bed as fell out of it," Nancy said, refusing to accept his to negativity.

Stan stood out of bed, slowly, not quite understanding why she was so cheerful, but no matter, he would be fine.

Nancy walked around the bed and looked straight at him. If she had been stood with her hands on her hips it would have done justice to her demeanor, like a school ma'am about to begin lessons.

Stan looked at her, sifting through his still sleepy mind for some kind of clever retort, before deciding it was still too early for that. She was often serious in nature, nothing too much, but aware of her responsibilities, and having no complaints, so he appreciated her being so upbeat.

As he stood up, Stan couldn't help himself, he just had to know. "OK, Nancy, what's so good today that has you all smiling?" Aware that it might sound like he was trying to be unreasonable, he softened his approach, looking directly back at her. Placing his arms around her he gently hugged her, smiling as best he could so early in the morning.

"Well, nothing really. I just want to see where Arthur is, and how he enjoyed his night on a blanket on a hard floor near the back door," Nancy said. The way she said it sounded cheerful and pleasant, even if her words sounded anything but.

Sounding like that, it made him feel bad for what he had done, but as much as emotionally he felt she might be right, in general terms he felt he was right; like a bank manager trying to decide if someone should have a loan, he placed a methodical approach to it, making a decision in his head, rather than his heart. Nancy stared at him, refusing to give him any inclination that she perhaps understood. He squirmed on the spot.

"How about we go have a look, and see how that little doggy fared during the night?" Nancy suggested.

Stan shrugged, realizing who was in charge. Before he could react Nancy turned and took his dressing gown from the back of the door, holding it out, ready for him to place on. He stepped into it, as if it were a straight jacket intended to snare him into her master plan.

Nancy opened the door quietly before slowly walking out. Stan followed, as if she had a hold of his hand, pulling him along. She didn't but he felt very much as if he were prey, being lead off for dinner, and he was the menu.

They both stood out on the landing, looking around. The bathroom door was closed, as was Abigail's room, with Billy's door closed to, still darkened from his thick curtains. When his curtains had been light, he often woke up so early it felt like they had only just got into bed, but the new ones worked a treat.

"Let's go see then," Nancy said, at which Stan nodded and they headed off. Down the stairs they went, and then down again, as Nancy stood closer to the back door, looking back at her beloved husband, a wry smile on her face.

The blanket wasn't how it had been left, originally in a corner, a neat oblong shape, enough to cover Arthur's needs. Now it was not merely ruffled up, but in a small pile, as if someone had wound it up, slapped it against a wall a few dozen times and dropped it right there, as if making a statement, with an unhappy look on their face.

"Maybe he's curled up underneath it?" Nancy suggested. How she spoke could have cut the air with a knife.

"Oh," Stan said, both confused and unhappy at the same time. "I wonder where he is?" he asked, looking at Nancy.

Nancy took his lead and shrugged. "No idea, gone for a walk outside maybe?"

Stan thought of saying something back, but he knew he was in the dog's house, unlike Arthur, and anything he said would just make it worse.

"I guess we will have to go find him," Nancy said, not waiting for him to reply. She turned and walked back up the stairs, only unknown to Stan she had begun to smile again, enjoying the moment.

Together they walked up the stairs, then along the hall, looking into the living room, opening cupboards just in case, then to the kitchen. Apart from the water bowl being empty, there was no sign of Arthur.

"I don't suppose," Stan began to say.

"What's that?" Nancy asked politely.

"That, he might have gotten into the cellar?" he asked, trying to sound thoughtful, but refusing to make eye contact with her.

"What?" Nancy snapped, clearly unhappy with the idea. She had her own thoughts on what was going on, but only then realized he could be right.

Instinctively Stan shrugged, which seemed to make it all the worse. If his lip had begun to quiver it would have put a seal on it, as he turned to a jelly of confusion and worry. He really was in the spotlight now.

"No, I'm sure," Stan tried to say.

"No, I hope not," Nancy said, before calming herself. "Perhaps he had gone into the bathroom, or our room, or," she began to say.

"Ohhh," Stan said, quickly walking back to the stairs. Nancy followed, half-mindful of what they might find.

Stan walked quickly ahead to the top, heading straight for Billy's room, brushing open the door and stepping in. He had a determined look on his face, one which suggested he knew that he was right.

As the door opened wide light from the hall spilled into the room, illuminating just enough to see Billy, fast asleep, looking lost to the world, in his own realms of slumber. Stan looked as best he could, peering into the darkness as his eyes adjusted. He was certain that Arthur would be laid there, on the bed, circled up at his son's feet, but he was nowhere to be found.

"No, he's not here either," Stan said, placing his hands on his hips. He looked at Nancy, his expression one of completed bafflement.

"Really?" Nancy asked, more baffled by her husband than the loss of their new dog.

Stan frowned. "What?" he asked.

"Look at bit closer," Nancy whispered.

Stan did as he was told, leaning in a little, finally thinking that Arthur had somehow snuggled under the covers, but no, he wasn't there either.

"Really, I sometimes wonder about you," Nancy said impatiently, moving past him. She knelt down while glancing at him, then towards Billy, lowering herself to the floor. Stan simply watched her, as if she were carrying out some kind of arcane practice which might elicit where the dog had magically gone to.

Finally, realizing his mind was frozen in wonder, Nancy grabbed Stan's hand before tugging him to join her on the floor. He followed suit, lowering down, until he too was sat on the thick carpet, peering ahead, into the darkness.

"What?" Stan said. Nancy wondered if he were doing it deliberately, that perhaps he just didn't want to acknowledge it.

"Look there, under the bed," Nancy said. As she too looked she let out a gasp, feeling a surge deep down of love for her son, and their new dog.

Finally it hit home to Stan, as his vision grew accustomed enough to see Arthur laid under the bed, wrapped up in clothes and toys, only his head was laid at an odd angle, pressed against the back wall.

"What, the," Stan began to say, intending to raise his voice to complain. Then he saw it, just what was going on, as it became clear that Billy's hand was extended down, cupping Arthur's ear, gently resting, holding each other while both were fast asleep.

Stan leaned back. "Wow," was all he said, both surprised as well as feeling some kind of emotion which he didn't understand. On the one hand he felt good about it, so happy for his son, but on the other he felt difficulty in seeing his son with a dog that until recently had been as much a stranger to him as his own mother had become.

"Ohhh," Nancy said, trying her best not to allow tears to flow, even if they were for joy. She leaned quickly towards Stan, wrapping her hands around his arm, snuggling in. "Aren't they wonderful," she said quietly.

"Yeah," Stan said, trying not to sound unhappy, but feeling as much.

"We should just leave them there, so they can enjoy their sleep," Nancy said, smiling broadly.

Stan looked at her sharply, intending to have his say.

"Is this some sort of group meet that I wasn't invited to?" a voice behind them asked, making them both jump.

"Muuum, Abigail's in my room again," Billy said without even having to open his eyes.

Both parents turned quickly to see Abigail stood behind then, wearing her school uniform. "Wow, you're up and ready early," Nancy suggested.

"Ha," Abigail said, turning to walk away. "Actually, you're all late, it's eight forty five, and school begins in fifteen minutes.

Panic hit them both, as Nancy struggled to stand up quickly enough. Stan rolled back, trying to get up but there wasn't enough room. The commotion woke Billy, who pushed down his covers looking on as his parents appeared to be having a contest to see who could look the daftest.

"Hold on, let me get up," Nancy said as she tried to push Stan back a bit.

"Yes, but I'm going to be late," Stan insisted as he too pushed against the bed, only to slip and fall back down again.

Billy might well have been half asleep, but he was awake enough to see how ridiculous they both were, so much that he began giggling.

The laughter and fuss finally woke up Arthur, who lifted his head up just in time to see Stan roll back on the floor, until the two of them came nose to nose, right beside each other. Stan looked at Arthur, annoyed with himself over his struggles. Arthur looked on, having no clue what was going on, but intrigued enough to lean forward a little, enough to lick the end of Stan's nose.

"Ha, he likes you, Dad," Billy shouted as he leaned over the bed, looking underneath.

Nancy giggled. "Careful, love, you don't want to fall," she said, enjoying the moment.

The suggestion was too much to resist, as Billy nudged himself just enough so that over he went, rolling into the floor as his mother half caught him, looking shocked.

Billy laughed so loud Arthur looked at him abruptly, before breaking out into a huge yawn, stretching as he did so.

"Good boy," Billy called loudly, giggling away to himself.

Stan struggled as best he could to stand up, with a dog trying to lick him, his son laughing and rolling around and his wife looking at it all as if they were all at a fun fair, enjoying the day together.

"Please, I need to eat," Stan pleaded as he held onto the edge of the bed for support.

"You can share Arthur's bone," Billy said, laughing ever louder. Arthur looked at him, ears up, eyes wide open, wondering what all the excitement was.

"Don't be silly, of course your dad can't share Arthur's bone," Nancy said, unable to resist the infectious laughter.

"Why not, Mum?" Billy asked as he patted Arthur on the head.

"Because Arthur hasn't got a bone," Stan replied in a deadpan voice as he walked out. Behind him he left Nancy and Billy to their laughter, only for Arthur to follow him as he walked away.

"What do you want now?" Stan asked, fully aware that Arthur was with him.

"A bone!" Nancy and Billy shouted together, before laughing even more.

What a start to the morning, they both thought. If life with Arthur was going to be like this every day, it was just going to be better than ever.

CHAPTER THIRTEEN

It all happened so fast. Abigail left, Stan simply went out of the room, began rushing around like it seemed was his way, and then Nancy dragged Billy out of bed while he was laughing about it. Then he went, and she went, and then they were all gone.

All except Arthur, who had sat at the top of the stairs, listening to them go, one by one, until he was alone. The door slammed, harder than it should have, making him jump. He waited, and then just for good measure waited a little longer.

The silence in itself was deafening, because to him and his sensitive hearing it had been madness, all chatter, laughter and shouting, and then nothing. He was so used to being out on the noisy streets, and then around the family, it seemed it was simply a world of noise.

Now what? In some ways Arthur had a mixed life, sometimes simple, sometimes complex. He was a strong dog, and could cope with most things, simply because he had no choice, but the problem was the not knowing how life would be, whether he would be alone and lonely, cold and unwanted, or would he be part of a family, and there would never be a dull moment, except now.

When Arthur had made his way into the house and hid, it had been a time of worry and concern; would they catch him, how would they react if they did find him? Their response had been odd, because it was so different in so many ways to what he had become used to. There was no shouting, no marching out, no anger, simply lots of hugs, joy, and laughter. He could be content, but something was wrong, something missing, yet he couldn't figure out what it was.

Arthur was unsure, but as always, determined to find out just what. He would go searching.

First up would be the kitchen. He stood up and wandered off, looking around, still unable to shake that sense that at any moment he would be shouted at. It seemed that if someone wasn't shouting, he wasn't doing it right.

Then it occurred to him, quite naturally, what he needed more than anything, and for a change it wasn't food. He needed to go out, not for long, not in that awful cold, but still he needed to do his business. He wondered what was going on. Did they not know he had to go out? They had gone out themselves, no doubt in his mind so that they could do their business, but what about him?

Still, Arthur was always inventive. He let out a quick pant, acknowledging his own needs, before merrily trotting along the hall towards the living room. At the door he peeked in, looking quickly around to see if anyone was still there. It would be so much simpler if there was, but of course no, he had been forgotten.

There it was, his salvation, what waited for him, in a corner, bright and green, looking so inviting. The potted plant wasn't intended for him to use, but he wasn't to know that, and besides what else was he supposed to do? It had worked before, and would do just fine again. Arthur walked ahead, circled around, trying to gain the best vantage point, before lifting his back leg. As he relieved himself, thankful in the knowledge that he could feel better, and that he was doing the right thing, watering the plant, he could have been forgiven for not realizing he was doing so on a plastic plant, having been put in place due to the real one dying, for who knew what reason. The plant was plastic, the soil was plastic, the flowers on it were plastic, and all of it was wet, but it didn't matter to Arthur, because he was a good dog.

Finally he was ready, so off he could go for the serious business of the day. He may well have only been a dog, but he still had his routine. If he had slippers and a newspaper he may well have indulged, because life was good and he had to do his things, each and every day.

Off he went, into the kitchen, sniffing the air expectantly, hopefully, like Aladdin's cave, full of treasures, only some hidden, some protected, and some he would have to work for. He had learned enough that water was placed there for him, so walked over to the bowl. It was different, no longer the simple dish that held hardly anything, not even the shiny metal thing which had replaced it. Now it was white, with pictures of dogs on it, full of crystal clear water, looking so inviting. He was so busy lapping it up, he didn't fully understand the nature of the change in the bowl, from dish, to tin, to proper dog bowl. To the family it was a signifier of his being welcomed in, a part of them, bit by bit adding his place in the home. To him it was a means to an end, because they were all that mattered to him, family, love, home, being safe. Oh, and not forgetting food, lots of food!

Arthur looked around a little, sniffing again, noticing the other bowl was empty. He walked over and licked it a little, enjoying the fine if meager taste. He could recall the night before when the bowl had been placed down and he had lapped up all the fine meat and kibble. It was wonderful, and licking the dish brought back memories, but he wanted more. Then as his mind wandered and he looked hopefully around, he saw it, a bone, right over in the corner. It was small, and lacking in meat, but it was most definitely a bone, and left close enough for him to pick up, without having to fight fridges or attack high tables for.

Arthur looked around, feeling that he was being tested, that if he dared to open his mouth and bite it, that at any moment someone would jump out and bark at him. Still, it was worth the risk. He lowered himself, picking it up with his mouth, ever so gently, as if it were an illusion, that if he did anything wrong it would go poof and disappear in a cloud of smoke. It didn't, but it tasted good. It was going to be his, but where, that was his question. He could pick it up and take it back underneath the bed, it was safe there, but it was dark, and difficult to see just what this bone was all about. He could stay there, eat it quickly, get it gone before anyone could object. For a fleeting moment he thought of maybe just dropping it and leaving it, the sensible option, but no. If dogs could laugh, Arthur would have done just that at the foolish thought, as if he would ever leave food behind. No chance.

Ignoring the possible outcomes, Arthur walked off with his bone, into the living room, right into the middle of the floor, amidst all the teddies, before plonking himself down. He laid, placed his front paws across the bone, and began his miniature feast. It tasted good; meat, bone, marrow, all the things a dog needed on a cold day, which happened to be in a warm house while laid on a plush carpet. Life wasn't so bad after all, but Arthur was too busy eating to think about it.

The problem with a good bone is that it doesn't last, like all food, which Arthur loved. His belly was full enough though, and the heating was on in the house. He allowed himself a single impolite burp, before looking up at the window. The skies were white, full of threatened snow, but he was safe and sound, and now all he needed was a sleep. Without further ado, he rolled over onto his side like a log rolling down a hill, allowing his legs to kick out, acknowledging his rotund belly. Darkness drifted over him as the quiet beauty of the house enveloped him. He was off to slumber town, to dream more of food and fun.

*

"Arthur, what are you doing?" a voice called abruptly. It never took much to wake him and make him react now. He had become so accustomed to others not wanting him there, it would be no surprise if his happiness could be broken by the sound of a strong voice and the look of a stern face. He sat quickly up, struggling at first, but then looked on wide-eyed and uncertain. The only thing that could be sure would be his reaction; he was ready to run again.

"You shouldn't bring bits of bone in here," Abigail said, as she walked into the living room, dropping her school bag on the floor near the door. Arthur sat looking at her, ready, but still hopeful. As she spoke his ears dropped, his shoulder slunk over, his tail unmoving. He felt confused.

Abigail kneeled down to pick up bits of bone, the leftovers of his minor feast. Arthur regretted the thought that the bits he was saving for later were being taken, but her unhappiness with him was of far greater concern.

Without speaking Abigail took the pieces of bone and walked out. Arthur remained in place wondering if he should follow her, what he might do to make her happy again. He thought to perhaps drop to the floor and show her his belly, that she might see his love and quickly give him a rub to say so.

Moments passed as his indecisiveness ate away at him. The longer he waited the more he thought he was in bigger trouble, but if he did anything he could make it worse. Feeling so torn, he just looked around, hoping there might be a kind face nearby, ready to comfort him, but there wasn't.

"I don't know, what are you like?" Abigail asked, walking back in again. The question might have made Arthur truly worry, until he spotted she was carrying a plate of sandwiches. He quickly stood up, ears up, eyes bright, tail sticking out, a clear look on his face of: *for me?*

"No, Arthur, this is my lunch," Abgail said, moving to sit on the sofa. Arthur turned with her every move, his head turning with the movements of the plate, as if it were attached by an invisible piece of thread. Abigail noticed him, smiling as he did. Having such little experience with dogs she had no idea of what to expect from him, as such everything he did was either a minor nuisance or a source of fun.

As she sat down, Arthur quickly made his way beside her. He sat once again, all eager eyes and happy, that he was ready for lunch, because breakfast had been so good. He sat, occasionally moving around on the spot, such was his excitement, only now his tail wagged, slapping against the side of the sofa, like a drummer in time with Abigail chewing her food.

"Nope," Abigail struggled to say, in between mouth full of cheese and tuna sandwiches. Each time she acknowledged him Arthur stood quickly up then sat back down, looking as if he intended to leap at her and gobble it all up. Every time Abigail smiled briefly, immediately followed by forced silence due to her anger at being amused by him.

"Silly dog," Abigail muttered, before mentally chastising herself for being negative towards him. He was though, to her, a silly dog, so why was she struggling to say it?

The food was just right, not too much, affecting her weight, which of course mattered now, but not so little that she would be hungry later. She picked at a corner of the bread, subconsciously thinking that if she ate small bites then she would remain petite and in great shape. As she picked a piece off, she noticed Arthur, still sat looking at her, but the moment she picked it off his ears pricked right up, and his excitement grew. As soon as she looked at him, his ears dropped and he sort of looked away.

Abigail placed the morsel into her mouth, chewing slowly while watching him. Arthur continued to look away, clearly unable to look her in the eye while she had food.

"Yum, lovely food," Abigail said, leaning towards him a little. She picked some more of the sandwich off, before holding it gently just out of reach of him. Arthur sort of stood, then sat, shifting around, before giving out a mild groan. Just as she was about the place the food into her mouth, she threw it quickly, watching Arthur as he caught it, quickly eating it.

He may well have been a silly dog, but he had his ways, and some to her were oddly cute. She could never have imagined seeing a dog as being cute before, but Arthur wasn't like most dogs, he had a certain unusual charm about him, a kindness and gentility which stood out.

Once again Abigail pulled a small piece of bread away, wrapped with some tuna and held it up, as if to eat it. She held it while looking slightly away, out of the corner of her eye, to see Arthur do his trick, ears up, eyes wide, staring straight at it as if it were a golden fleece. Quickly she turned back to look at him, as his ears dropped, he blinked quickly, turning slightly away, lowering his head. Once again she looked away, then back again quickly, then away, seeing just enough to notice his ears bounce up and down, as he turned his head to her and away and back. Finally it was too much, as Arthur yapped at her loudly, clearly annoyed by her playfulness.

It was just too funny, causing her to laugh about it. She stopped suddenly, annoyed that she had devoted so much of her time and effort to such a silly dog. Even so, she still threw a tiny piece off to him which, adept as ever, he caught without having to move from his spot.

"What?" Abigail asked as she finished the last of her sandwich. She took a drink from a beaker nearby, all the while keeping her eyes pinned on him. Arthur just looked back as they continued to stare at each other. His only interest was the possibility of more food, but to her she allowed her mind to wander, to think of things he had seen and where he had been.

"Got to go," Abigail said suddenly, at which Arthur stood up, wondering what they would be doing together.

"Don't want any silly dog looking at me," Abigail muttered, quickly standing up. Taking her school bag she walked out of the living room without bothering to look back. Arthur followed her every move, waiting, thinking that any moment she would look back at him and speak, offer some kind words, perhaps even more food. She didn't, instead walking out of the room and away.

Arthur walked slowly to the door, stopping just enough so that he could see her go. Still she didn't look back, but she was aware he was there, she could just tell.

Abigail got to the stairs, preparing to descend before stopping, hesitating, but she had no idea why. All her thoughts were on going back to school, meeting her friends, doing her thing. "No time for foolish dogs," she muttered, quite nonchalant about it all.

Quite what made her turn and glance towards Arthur, she had no idea, but she did. Arthur wasn't so much stood in the hall watching her, as leaning his head, slightly sideways, watching her every movement. Everything he did made her think he was silly, she was annoyed with herself for even thinking of him at all when she was so busy.

"What are you looking at?" Abigail asked, talking to Arthur. He looked at her, turning his head, as if confused by what she might be saying. He couldn't read her, had no idea what her intentions were, whether she was being kind or offering him something, or perhaps telling him to go away.

"Silly dog," Abigail said again, ready to turn away.

Both looked at each other, each unsure of what the other wanted or was thinking. Just as she was about to call him a name again, before walking away down the stairs, she turned fully, feeling an odd impulse, she walked quickly over to him, dropped to her knees and hugged him.

Arthur felt shocked, surprised by her sudden change. As she had approached he had panicked, wondering if she was going to shout at him, to order him away, perhaps to do something that even he couldn't imagine. What she did was such a surprise he didn't know what to do.

Abigail kneeled beside him, wrapped her arms around him and pulled him in tightly, hugging him as much as she could.

Pulling away slightly, she looked in his eyes, which made him bashful, as he struggled to look into hers. His tail wagged ferociously, uncontrollably, feeling a kind of joy he had forgotten. He wagged so much his whole body shook as he bounced around in her arms.

For her part, Abigail couldn't stop herself from smiling. His excitement was always infectious, but how he was now, with her, seeming so happy simply to be with her, being hugged by her, it made her feel in a way she hadn't in recent times. She still felt torn, part of her wanting to push him away and make fun, but she just couldn't, wouldn't allow herself to be so unkind.

Once again Abigail cuddled Arthur, as he pushed himself into her, closing his eyes, feeling the warmth, the love, all the things he had missed for far too long. It had been a while, finding his way in the home, one person at a time it seemed, but gradually he was feeling increasingly settled, as if it might just be his forever home after all.

"Right, got to go, for real this time," Abigail said suddenly, aware that time for her lunch break was ticking away. It had certainly been different, she was sure of that. As she stood up she noticed all of Arthur's fur stuck to her uniform, shaking her head in mock annoyance. As she walked away once again, brushing herself down she didn't look back, she didn't have to, she just knew what was coming.

Arthur looked at her as she walked away, waiting for that turn, perhaps for her to once again rush over to her, more hugs, but it didn't happen. This time she walked down the stairs and was leaving, leaving him. Quickly he jumped ahead, racing down the stairs, chasing after her.

Abigail laughed. She had fully expected him to do something, but not so excitable. As she got to the back door she stopped and once again looked at him.

"You can't come with me, Arthur, sorry," she said, opening the door, at which he shot outside. The moment he got out, into the bitter cold, the wet underfoot, he regretted it, reminded again just how cozy it all was inside.

"Arthur, get back in, you can't be out."

She had no idea that he very much agreed with her, that the last thing he wanted was to be outside, in all that snow and ice, but he was busy, for just a moment.

"Come on, Arthur," Abigail said as Arthur ran around in circles, as if he were looking for something.

"Please, Arthur," she said clapping her hands together, as if that might work. "You have to," she began to say, at which Arthur stopped and assumed the position. Abigail looked on, pulling a face at him. "Oh, Arthur, I'm not cleaning that up. Someone else can do that. Billy can, cos he's, well he's with you," Abigail continued, not daring to look.

The moment he finished, Arthur sprang up, shook his body and ran towards her.

"Right," Abigail began to say, ready to pat him on the head, or something similar, but he shot straight past her, in through the door and was gone.

"I guess you're not that daft, are you?" Abigail asked as she closed and locked the door. Looking quickly through the glass there was no sign of him. "Nope, not daft at all," she said, walking away.

Arthur ran up the stairs, fully aware of the warmth, which he loved. He looked back a moment, wondering if she would follow, or whether she too had to do her business. Time passed and silence descended again, apart from his heavy breathing. There seemed only one thing left to do now, and that was the next best thing to eating.

Arthur wandered down the hall to the living room, looked around at the teddies and thought of perhaps having a play, but he was alone, and for the first time in ages realized he missed his new family. Quietly he let out a small whimper, hoping someone would hear him. He knew better, but felt the need anyway. As always, he was a strong dog, and would get through it, and as always he was a hopeful dog.

Of course he wouldn't sleep with the teddies, as much as they offered some kind of presence to snuggle up to. Arthur wandered off, back up the stairs and into Billy's room. Lowering himself, he crawled under the bed, got as comfortable as he could, and drifted off into an aimless sleep.

CHAPTER FOURTEEN

When the noise began, it did so only slightly at first, then grew louder, until it was so loud that Arthur had no choice but to see what all the fuss was about. There were voices, banging about, music playing, as if the place were filled with dozens of newcomers, perhaps to see the new dog.

Arthur struggled to make his way out from under the bed, no longer afraid of being seen. He stretched awkwardly, before letting out a huge yawn. The sleep had been good, and unusually for him seemingly dreamless. Maybe he had no more worries to think about, real or unreal. Time would tell.

Then came the sound of Billy's voice, calling out to Abigail, who called back at him. Then there was Nancy, calling to all of them, so no time to waste. Arthur ran out of the room and down the stairs, wanting to see what all the fuss was about, but also simply to see them all, and if he was lucky to share some love with them too.

"Here he is," Nancy called, just as she was removing her coat. Arthur bounded along to see them all in the kitchen. As he entered he saw Billy sat on a chair at the table, as he jumped up to greet him. Abigail was stood by the counter, looking like she was eating a carrot. She looked back at him, offering a knowing glace, but she would never tell of their little secret, what she really felt.

There would be no such qualms with Billy, as he dropped quickly to the floor, grabbing Arthur around the neck, hugging him as tightly as he could.

"Careful, love, don't hurt him," Nancy said.

"Yeah, you don't want to get covered in fur, hugging him," Abigail said, mock wiping herself down. Nancy looked at her, laughing at what she meant.

"He's my baby," Billy said, giggling to himself.

Arthur loved every second of it, enjoying the happiness in the house, soaking up all the fuss and love. All he needed was his food and life would be perfect.

"What's all this fuss about then?" Stan asked, walking into the kitchen. He had come indoors and gone straight into the living room, but wanted to see what was going on.

"It's Arthur, he's happy to see us," Nancy said, leaning over to kiss her husband on the cheek. Usually they would smile at each other, hug a little, chatter about the day just gone, before getting on with tea and the rest of the evening. Tonight was different, Stan was different, simply looking at Arthur, seeming thoughtful, pensive even.

"You alright, love?" Nancy asked, taking a gentle hold of his arm.

Stan shrugged. "Yeah, I'm fine, just tired, that's all."

Arthur wagged his tail ever more upon seeing Stan, unable to control his excitement. Everyone looked at them both, waiting for Stan to at least say hello, or perhaps hug him, but instead he simply turned and walked out.

"Dad, what about the pooch?" Abigail called.

Nancy looked at her smiling. "I thought you weren't too fond of the dog?" she asked.

"I'm not, they're very annoying," Abigail replied, before walking over to Arthur, who was still sat waiting, patiently. She leaned over, kissed him on the head and walked out, smirking at her mother.

"Hey, dogs don't like kisses," Billy called, taking a hold of Arthur, hugging him even more.

"Really?" Nancy asked, leaning over to kiss Arthur gently on the top of his head. He was loving it, lapping up all the attention, but it didn't compare to a nice plate of food.

Billy wrinkled his nose at the thought of kissing a dog. "He's a bit smelly for a kiss," he said, before giving him a peck anyway.

"He shouldn't be smelly, he's had a bath," Nancy said.

"He smells of Abigail," Billy said, as he stood up and walked out. Nancy looked at Arthur, who looked straight back at her.

"Whatever that means, Arthur, I think it's a good thing," she said, before patting him on the head and following the others. Arthur stood up, looked around at his food bowl, still empty and sighed. These people, they just didn't appreciate when a dog had needs.

Finally Arthur decided he didn't want to be the one left behind, and no longer wanted to be alone, so he too wandered off to see where everyone had gone. They were all in the living room, sat around, except Billy who was running around in circles holding a toy in his hand.

"I guess we had best get started," Stan said, standing up again. It felt odd to Arthur, as every time he entered a room with Stan, he walked out again. Instinctively he felt something was wrong. If he could have talked he would have asked what the matter was, but he couldn't so simply gave his best *I'm cute* look in Stan's direction, and waited.

"Time for what?" Nancy asked.

"I shall be back in a moment," Stan said, at which he walked out without bothering to look at Arthur.

"Maybe he's gone for a jog," Abigail said, at which Nancy laughed.

"Maybe he's gone to the toilet," Billy suggested, not bothering to stop running around in circles. He had noticed that Arthur was watching his every move now, so decide to add engine noises to his model airplane, enjoying being the center of attention.

Before Nancy could have her say, Stan walked in struggling with two large boxes. "Oh, I completely forgot about that," she said.

"What are they?" Abigail asked.

"Wow, memory of a goldfish or what?" Nancy mocked. She stood up to take one of the boxes Stan was carrying. Together they walked over to the corner, placing them down.

Billy stopped his fun, intrigued by what was going on. Even Arthur was curious, walking over to sniff the boxes. They smelled a little musty, reminiscent of the cellar, a place he certainly didn't want to end up in again.

Stan leaned over, pulled off a strip of sellotape and opened the flaps of the top box. Then he produced a large bundle of shiny Christmas tinsel, dropping it onto the floor.

"It's that time of year again, or had you forgotten?" he asked, looking mildly pleased with himself.

"Oh, well done you," Nancy offered, helping to remove decorations.

"Well, time is getting on, getting close to celebrations, so I had been planning on doing this a while. With all the fuss recently, I just forgot until now."

Arthur took another step closer. He faintly recognized the colors and shapes, bringing back vague memories of good times and bundles of fun. He also remembered her. He remembered too how much he missed her, her smell, her kindness, just being there, every single day, until.

As soon as they all knew what the boxes were for, everyone piled in, all except Arthur, who still wanted his dinner, but it was fun to watch anyway.

Billy pulled more tinsel out as Abigail took smaller boxes of lights and unraveled them. Nancy brought out tubs of baubles, as Stan unpacked a long narrow box.

"Are we having a real tree this year?" Billy asked excitedly.

Stan, Nancy and Abigail all looked at him directly. "No," they said in unison.

"Oh," Billy said, surprised by the reaction.

"Because, I don't think it's a good idea to have a real tree in here, with a new dog, just in case he thinks it's his new place to cock his leg and, well, you know what," Stan said.

Billy giggled.

Little did anyone know that Arthur had found a good place already, but no doubt in time they would find out.

"So what are we using?" Nancy asked, at which Stan immediately withdrew a long silvery bundle from the box he was holding.

"Oh no, not that thing, it's hideous," Nancy said quickly.

Stan dropped the box, before beginning to pull out branches from the plastic tree. It was old, completely silver, and small.

"Oh no, not that again," Abigail said, pulling a face.

"I love it," Billy said, watching as his dad gathered and attached three plastic feet and stood it up. It was small, but still far bigger than him, and shiny to boot.

"Do you like it, Arthur?" Billy asked, ignoring the look on his mother's and sister's faces.

Arthur simply watched, ears up, eyes bright, enjoying every moment of it. It seemed like it was playtime, full of happiness and joy. At least to him it was.

"See, he loves it," Stan said, ignoring the mocking looks he got back.

Accepting the way it was, everyone jumped in, helping to decorate the room and the tree. Even if the tree was old, and all silver, and plastic, it was still part of the build up to Christmas, which made everyone excited.

Finally it was done. Halfway through Billy had sat down, feeling tired, followed shortly after by Abigail, feeling tired and distracted by television. Stan and Nancy continued, got it all done, because that is what parents do, for their children, and each other.

"Who wants to do the honors?" Stan asked.

"For what?" Abigail asked, lazing back on the sofa, barely able to concentrate on what was being said.

"I'll do it," Billy called, not having any idea what his father was on about.

"Come on then," Nancy said, at which Billy ran up. Stan pointed to the electrical socket.

"Oh, switching on the lights," Billy said, barely able to contain himself.

"Oh, no, I wanted to do it," Abigail chimed in, looking disappointed.

"Well, you were asked," Nancy said. She was right, but it didn't help.

"Never mind, you can put the fairy on top of the tree," Stan said as Billy flicked the switch.

"I guess I will have to," Abigail said, trying to sound as if she wasn't impressed. Though she wouldn't admit it, she was excited to be able to do it.

The fairy was placed on top, after which they all stood back. The place was always comfortable, but now with it all lit up and covered in glitter and tinsel, the place looked magical.

Arthur had laid on the floor, but remained watching the entire time. It was more than he had ever seen before. With the lady, she had always kept a small tree, and a few things around the place, but nothing ever so bright and welcoming as this. He could sense the excitement and energy in the room, and the happiness they all shared. Nothing could spoil it for him, so he hoped.

"Well done, everyone, and well done, Arthur," Nancy said. Everyone nodded, agreeing.

"Wait, what? What did Arthur do to help?" Abigail asked.

"He remembered it, and got the boxes out, it's all because of Arthur, thank you very much," Nancy said, patting Stan on the shoulder. He looked at her, bemused.

"Mum," Abigail said.

"Yes, love," Nancy replied.

"Have you gone a bit daft? What are you on about?" Abigail continued.

"Arthur's the dog, not Dad," Billy said as he was busy gently flicking Arthur's ear.

Nancy laughed. "Well, clearly you don't know where Arthur got his name, do you?" she asked, struggling to contain herself.

"No," Stan whispered.

Abigail shook her head. "No, I just thought Nan gave him that name, no idea where from."

"Well," Nancy began to say.

"Seriously?" Stan asked, his mouth wide open at the thought.

"You don't probably know this, but your dad's middle name is Arthur," Nancy said, giggling away happily.

"No way," Billy shouted, laughing with her.

"Yes, and I believe she called the dog after her son," Nancy replied, looking at Stan while laughing.

"You don't know that," Stan insisted. "It could have been for anything."

Nancy shrugged, enjoying the fun.

"Here boy, come here, Arthur," Abigail called, clapping her hands. Arthur stood up, walking over to her, feeling merry about all the happiness in the room, even if he had no clue why.

"No, not you, sweety," Abigail said, looking at Arthur as he sat beside her, waiting for his cuddle. "I meant that Arthur. Here, boy," she continued, pointing towards her dad.

"Funny," Stan said in a low voice, frowning at her.

"Hold on a second," Abigail insisted, before running out of the room.

"Hello, Arthur," Billy said, looking at his dad.

"Now Billy, you don't call us by our names," Stan said.

"Sorry, Stan, er, I mean, Dad," Billy replied playfully.

Before anything else could be said Abigail bounded in, holding a handful of dog biscuits and a chewing stick.

"Oh, has he been a good boy then?" Nancy asked, looking at Arthur the dog.

"Yes," Abigail replied, smiling. "Right, catch the biscuit," she called, holding a pink round one up, before throwing it. The biscuit flew through the air, bouncing gently off Stan's head and onto the floor. Arthur jumped up quickly, grabbing it, thinking he had been a good boy and deserved it.

Nancy burst out laughing again, hugging Stan for being such a good sport. Abigail laughed uncontrollably, as Billy walked over, patting his father on the back, laughing too.

Stan looked at them, wondering what was so funny. "I shall go and get a drink, I think," he said, walking out of the room.

"Good boy," Billy said, at which he, Nancy and Abigail all laughed.

As Abigail sat down, Arthur spotted she had a chewing stick for him. He stood up, wagging his tail at her, excited as could be. He almost bounced he was so excited that he might get a treat.

"You want some more then?" Abigail asked. Arthur duly bounced some more, wagging his tail even more.

Nancy and Billy watched as Arthur finally sat, only this time he did what he had been taught to do, but no one until now had bothered to ask; he held up a paw, as if to say please can I have it?

"Oooh," Abigail cooed. She held out the chewing stick for him, but as he made to take it she quickly pulled it away. Arthur stopped, pulling back a little, but refusing to give up.

"Poor Arthur, don't torment him," Nancy said.

Once again Abigail held out the stick for him, only now he approached it slowly, opening his mouth gently, expecting her to snatch it away. She held the stick, just slightly pulling it away, but not far enough that he might become frustrated. Arthur leaned in to her, moving ever so slowly, mouth carefully open, as he nudged her for the stick. She held it just close to his mouth, as if they were both moving and working in slow motion.

Arthur tried to nibble on the stick, but Abigail moved slightly away, until he was holding it, but not trying to eat it. It seemed to be a frozen tug of war between them both, but neither of them making an effort.

"Good boy, Arthur," Billy said, watching on in awe at him sat holding the stick with Abigail, but refusing to bite or take it.

Finally Abigail gave in, allowing him to take it. Arthur took the chewing stick and walked away, laying on the carpet to enjoy it.

"What a lovely dog," Abigail said. Nancy looked at her, full of surprise, having never seen her so emotional about an animal before. She was pleased to see them getting on.

Nancy looked around, only then noticing Stan stood in the doorway, leaning on the frame. He had been watching the whole time.

"He really is lovely, isn't he?" Nancy asked.

Stan shrugged, before walking out again. "Time for supper, I think, and Arthur hasn't eaten properly yet," he called back. It was true, he was right again, but clearly things weren't quite right.

CHAPTER FIFTEEN

It was Christmas Eve, and all through the house, nothing was stirring, not even a mouse. Arthur was though, he was chewing a large bone. A blanket had been placed on the floor for him to lay on, so as not to make a mess with it, and he was clearly enjoying every bit of it. He was quite a refined dog, at least until the streets had taught him a thing or two about being hungry, and the need to find a meal as and when, then his top hat and tails had slipped a little. It was a good bone, large, some meat on it, well-cooked, and just the way he liked it. He was a lucky dog.

Stan was pottering around in the kitchen, doing very little, but keeping busy with it. Finally he had finished work for the holidays, and had in mind all the things that needed preparing for the big day ahead. There would be food to be prepared, presents were already sorted, decorations up, and food and drink needed for the entire holidays all bought in. All that remained was a distraction, to smother the endless doubt he had in his mind, the ongoing nagging that ate away at his thoughts. The only problem was he couldn't figure out where it was coming from. It was an annoyance he could do without, because he loved Christmas.

For Arthur, the bone was a good one that helped fill his belly, and filled his heart with joy. He could sense the love in the room with him, and the warmth of the place made him feel settled and at home. Still, he knew there were one or two things out of place, he could just sense it, like most dogs. Arthur was a hopeful dog, always positive, always trying to be happy and wanting the same for others too, perhaps even cats as well. Sometimes.

Once he had had enough, he stood up, shook himself, starting at his head before descending down until his whole body shook and his back legs bounced off the carpet with the force of it.

Billy was sat on the floor nearby, watching television, a live action Peter Pan, a story which he always loved. As good as it was, it couldn't compare to Arthur when he was doing something funny. Billy laughed to himself how unusual Arthur could be, doing the oddest of things and yet so much fun with it.

As Billy laughed, Nancy lowered her magazine which she was reading to look to see what all the fuss was about. She caught sight of Arthur, as he too caught sight of her looking straight at him. The two stared at each other, waiting for the other to say or do something. Nancy chuckled to herself over it, how he was simply looking at her, as if he were about to start a conversation over something. Perhaps he might discuss the chilly weather, or even what Santa might bring him as a present, another bone perhaps. Arthur really did have his way, and seemed so human at times.

Abigail as always had been on the telephone, talking to one of her friends. She was sat in a corner, lounging around, enjoying the peace and quiet. Things were changing for her, in life and at school, and it was nice to just switch off from things, to look forward to the presents and Christmas dinner, not to mention endless hogging of the telephone.

"Mum, will I be getting a mobile phone for Christmas?" Abigail asked.

Nancy looked at her. "We'll have to see what Santa thinks, whether you've been good or not," she replied.

Abigail frowned. "Funny."

Arthur suddenly flopped down hard onto the carpet like a thrown sack of spuds. All three looked at him, wondering what he was doing. Arthur rolled onto his back, lessening the weight on his full belly, before rolling around, shifting sideways, this way and that, as if half curling. He appeared to be scratching his back, but at the same time his mouth hung open, and he made silly noises, enjoying every minute of it.

"What's he doing, Mum?" Abigail asked.

Nancy shrugged, smiling at Arthur as he scrunched around on his back, this way and that.

Billy suddenly rolled over, assuming the same position, arms and legs in the air, doing the same. "Oh, that feels good," he said.

Arthur stopped what he was doing, looking at the young boy beside him, staring at him. Billy looked back, as the two made clear eye contact. It was fine, they had an itch, needed to scratch, so began again to waddle around, fluffing on the carpet, both on their backs, rolling and shifting, enjoying every moment of it.

Nancy smiled at them both, and seeing as it was Christmas Eve, she could let her hair down, have a little silly seasonal fun. Dropping the magazine to the table beside her she pushed forward and rolled out onto the carpet, turning onto her back. Abigail watched in shock, amazed at what they were doing. Her mother, brother and the dog, all rolling around on their backs, laughing.

Stan finished what he was doing, washing some vegetables and cleaning down the table. His thoughts were interrupted by laughter coming from the living room. At first he imagined it was the television, but the knocking and chattering sounded too close to be that. It was too much; he had to go see for himself. Removing his apron with the words Kitchen Dad written on it, he turned and walked out of the kitchen, into the hall and to the living room.

The moment Stan walked through the door Arthur once again immediately ceased what he was doing, to look upside down at him. His chops were hanging open, his front paws bent in front of him, tail wagging slowly, rubbing the carpet.

Nancy and Billy looked at him, copying Arthur, stopping in their tracks, both on their backs, hands in the air, looking like the dog.

"Right, OK," Stan said, looking perplexed. "Am I missing something?" he asked.

"Yes, Dad," Abigail said, quickly shuffling off the chair, onto the floor. She laid on her back, pushed her hands into the air and began shuffling around. "Can't beat them, join them," she said.

Nancy and Billy began doing so again, moving around, all three laughing. It was such a surprise that Arthur stopped what he was doing, rolled upright and looked at them all, in as much shock as Stan. Still, it was fun.

"I'm not sure," Stan began to say, at which Arthur suddenly leapt up. He just couldn't resist, so off he went, front paws low, yapping quickly, looking at them, before jumping sideways, left then right.

"Go on, boy," Billy shouted, which was just the starting shot Arthur needed, as he bounded away, running like mad across the living room floor. He ran from one end to the next, tongue hanging out, eyes wide, looking as if he were in the race of his life. Nancy, Billy and Abigail stopped what they were doing, watching him rush around like his bottom was on fire.

"Careful," Stan said as Arthur ran past him. He shot along the hall and up the stairs. All that they could hear were the thumps of Arthur's paws as he sprinted for dear life along and back again. Then he came again, thudding down the stairs, off into the kitchen.

"I think perhaps he needs a walk," Nancy said, laughing.

"Or a run," Abigail said, enjoying every second of it.

"We all can," Billy said excitedly, as a kitchen chair clattered to the floor as Arthur barged into it. He stopped quickly, before once again pouncing on invisible air and running out.

"Now that's," Stan began to say as Arthur ran quickly past him, down the hall, and back, turning quickly into the living room. Stan moved as fast as he could, out of the way, but not fast enough as Arthur crashed into him, hitting him full on in the legs. It was so unexpected that Stan dropped as if he had been cut in half, collapsing to the ground, crashing with a loud thud as he hit the carpet.

Arthur stopped what he was doing, fully aware of what he had done. Nancy let out a gasp, as she quickly tended to Stan, looking to make sure he wasn't hurt. Billy and Abigail looked on in shock.

"Are you hurt? Are you alright, love?" Nancy asked, placing a supportive hand on his shoulder.

Stan sat up a little. "Yeah, I'm fine," he said, sounding more unhappy than hurt. "Stupid dog," he said, which shocked them all. He had never been the kind of man to lose his temper, and certainly not one to talk in such a way.

"Stanley," Nancy whispered, calling him by his full name, which was clearly much more personal to them both. He looked at her, aware of the problem, but somehow unable to shift his mood.

Arthur had stopped running, stood with his head bowed, aware of the change in the situation. He looked on, eyes narrowed, fearful for the outcome.

Neither Billy or Abigail spoke, except to stand up and move to sit on the sofa. Whatever was going to happen, it might not be good.

Stan slowly pulled himself to his feet, brushing himself down. Nancy followed, holding his arm, looking at him with a wistful smile. She thought of making a joke of it, to lighten the mood, it was Christmas Eve after all, but decided to wait.

"I think," Stan began to say, at which everyone held their breath. "We had better take him out for a walk," he continued, looking at them all. It seemed as if crisis averted, all was fine again.

"Can I come?" Billy asked. Stan nodded.

Both went to get their coats and shoes on, as Nancy got Arthur's lead. It was a good idea, a chance to cool down and start again. It had been fun, but perhaps got a little out of hand.

Finally ready, Billy took Arthur's lead and looked at him, smiling. "Come on, boy, let's go," he said, deliberately not using the word *run* in case he did just that.

Together they went down, as Stan opened the back door. Nancy followed, watching them step out into the night cold, as brittle snow surrounded them. The skies were again clear, lending a harsh frost across everything. The place was silent, as few dared venture out into such extremes, but Arthur needed his time out, and so off they went.

"Be careful, it's a bit slippery," Stan said, looking towards Billy as he held the lead tightly. Arthur stopped to sniff but struggled to make any impression, given the frigid night air.

Abigail had joined them, standing just behind Nancy, not so foolish enough to join them in the trek across what seemed like an Arctic wasteland.

"We'll walk across the grass, avoid that path in case we fall," Stan said, aware that he should have cleared the snow well before then.

"OK, Dad," Billy said, breathing out heavily so that he could see long streams of white vapor from his breath. It was testament to just how cold it would be.

"Right, come on," Stan said, turning quickly. As he did his foot slipped a little, causing him to stop. He looked down to see the discolored snow, dark and muddy. The smell became immediately obvious.

"Oh, wow, what's this," Stan asked, before realizing it was something left behind by a dog.

"Oh no," Abigail said quickly, aware of what had happened.

"What's up?" Nancy asked, turning towards her daughter.

"Arthur, he made a mess out there and I forgot to clean it up," she said, horrified at the prospect of what might happen.

"Arthur," Stan shouted.

Arthur looked quickly to where he was being called, still excited over being outside. Stan wiped his foot as best he could, before walking quickly over towards him.

"What is this? What have you done?" Stan stormed, shouting now. Arthur cowered back, afraid at being shouted at in such a way, by someone he thought cared about him. He slunk away, behind Billy's legs, peering out from behind.

Stan shook his head. "Let's just go," he said, walking off. Billy followed, tugging on Arthur's lead. Arthur held fast, at first refusing to walk, until finally giving in, knowing he had to. He felt reluctant, what with the cold, being so dark, but mostly how he sensed problems building. Deep down he knew what it was.

Billy and Stan walked off, with Arthur following behind, ensuring to keep his distance from Stan. Nancy and Abigail watched them go, before closing the door. They looked at each other, aware there was a problem, but it was the wrong time of year to be having it, and neither wanted to think that it could be anything but perfect for their new dog.

Walking ahead, Stan only stopped for the main road, looking back to ensure Billy and Arthur were with him. The roads were covered in ice and snow, thick long tracks stretching either way along under the railway arch. Across the way was the park, littered with newly-rolled giant snowballs and snowmen created in various places. Arthur was eager to get there, to go and sniff around, but he too was distracted by the tension between them.

"Right, cross, nothing coming," Stan said, stepping carefully out onto the icy road. Billy thought to make a joke of it, that they didn't want to fall over, but decided not to in case it made things worse.

As they walked across and entered the park, neither spoke, stopping only occasionally so Arthur could sniff or do something quickly.

With each step they took, it seemed to Billy that things appeared worse, that he needed to know, was everything going to be alright with Arthur? He wanted to ask, but didn't dare for what he might hear. He could just keep quiet and expect it would be all fine.

"Come on, let's go this way," Stan said, at which Billy broke out into a run. Arthur looked up, surprised by the sudden burst of activity, realizing he might get left behind, so followed suit, breaking out into a run. Stan watched as Billy ran one way, and Arthur another, as the lead stretched out.

"Hold on," Stan said, sounding louder than he had intended.

"Arthur," Billy shouted, tugging on the lead while trying to pull back.

All Arthur could hear was shouting, with the forceful tugging of his lead. He moved away, tried to wriggle out, before looking at Stan. The appearance on his face looked dark, so unhappy, perhaps he had made a mistake, the sounds, the noise, the shouting, there it all was again. Now he knew.

Arthur struggled more, at which Billy shouted back to stop, pulling the lead.

"No, don't," Stan tried to say, too late as Arthur finally slipped his head from the collar. He waited barely a second before his mind was made up, knowing what he had to do. It had been there all along, in his mind, in his instincts, the smells, the sounds, the way it seemed.

"Dad," Billy shouted, wide-eyed, afraid of seeing their new dog without a collar or lead, free to do as he pleased.

"No, Arthur," Stan shouted, reaching out quickly, wanting to take a hold of him before the inevitable happened.

Of course, Arthur was far too wily for that, too experienced. He had been there before, others doing what he feared wasn't right. It wouldn't happen again, as he turned abruptly and ran, sprinting away for everything he could.

"Arthur," Billy shouted, trying to run after him, but it was too late. He disappeared into the darkness at the far corner of the park before Stan could even react. In the bitter winter night he was gone, off onto the streets once again.

"Dad," Billy cried, running to Stan, wrapping his arms around him.

"Oh no," Stan whispered. He thought to immediately go looking for him, but knew it was too late and too cold for his son to be out so long.

"I'll go look for him, but it's too cold for you to be out," Stan said, hugging Billy tightly. He could feel the sobs of his son as he cried. "I'll look for him, Billy, come on," he said, before taking his hand and walking back.

It was too much for Billy, his tears and grief making it impossible for him. Stan stopped, before picking him up, cradling him in his arms. He knew time was short, he had to get out and look for him.

Stan opened the back door wide. "Nancy," he shouted, putting Billy down into the bottom hallway.

Nancy and Abigail came running. Nancy stopped, looking at him, then Billy as he cried. "What, what's happened?" she asked hurriedly.

"It's Arthur, he got off his lead, and ran," Stan said. Nancy took Billy in her arms, pulling him in.

"Did he come home again?" Billy asked, full of hope.

"No, love, not this time, I'm so sorry," Nancy replied, at which Billy clung to her even tighter.

"What are you going to do?" Nancy asked, looking up at Stan.

"I'll go look for him," he replied.

"Billy, you go up with your sister, I'll be there in a moment. I'm sure we'll find him," Nancy offered, doing her best to comfort him.

"I want to go look," Billy pleaded.

"No, son, I'll be quicker by myself," Stan said, trying his best to sound comforting.

Abigail stepped forward, taking Billy's hand. "Come on, let's go up, Dad will sort it," she said.

Reluctantly he finally gave in, walking slow with her up the stairs.

Nancy looked at Stan. "What's going on? It just seemed like you were never happy having him here?" she asked.

Stan shook his head. "I know, it's not that. It's just," he began to say, trailing off.

"It's just because he was your mum's dog," she said quietly. Stan nodded.

"I guess I've just not dealt with it," he said, head down.

"Where will he go?" Nancy asked.

"I think I know. I'll go, I'll find him," he said. Nancy hugged him, knowing he would do his best.

Without saying anything else, Stan leaned in, took his car keys from the wall rack, hugged his wife and walked off. Nancy closed the door, leaning against it inside, thinking to herself. She wondered what it might be like if he didn't find him, but she knew he would do everything he could, because he loved them, and would do whatever it took.

CHAPTER SIXTEEN

Stan climbed into the car and fired up the engine, barely waiting for the screen to clear before he drove out. He had thought to perhaps simply walk the streets looking for Arthur, but deep down he had an idea of what it might come to. There would be two places he could look for him, and intended to try them both.

It was the last thing he had imagined doing on such a night. He knew they should all be indoors, warm, happy, and excited for the wonderful occasion ahead. He always accepted his responsibilities in life, and having such a loving family it was worth every moment and everything he ever had to do.

Turning left from the driveway he passed under the bridge, along and left at the roundabout. He thought of how things were, allowing his mind to wander, thinking of Arthur, and who he had come from. It was like a brick wall in his mind, that beyond it lay something unbearable to think about. He couldn't climb over it; he had to break it down. Since Arthur had arrived the barrier to his emotions had been chipping away, slowly eroding, as much as he had tried to fight it, or at least ignore it. Now, everything had come to a head, there would be no turning back, no avoiding confronting the things that were wrong in his life. It was all about him, but focused entirely on Arthur, and what he represented.

The thought that he might not find Arthur never entered his mind. It seemed inevitable to him that he would. What struck him most, and most affected him was what he would do when they met up, what he might have to do once and for all.

The air was so cold out that a fine white mist hung around the roads ahead. The roads were treacherous for driving but passable. He was thankful that the first place he intended to try wasn't far, but he still felt sick in the pit of his stomach that he ever had to go back. The thought brought it back to him, how he was, how he was dealing with things. He realized deep down that he wasn't.

The traffic lights near his destiny were green and the large gates open, allowing him to drive straight in. The place was dark, no lights at all, which made sense. He slowly drove the car in, stopping close to the large entrance. Given the time of year there would be no one around, except perhaps others in mourning.

Stan climbed out of the car, immediately looking for Arthur. All of his attention was on that, but a part of him knew he wouldn't be there. It seemed as if fate were driving them to a certain place, as if Arthur had always been destined to go where he probably was, and for the first time Stan found himself hoping he would be there. If not, he feared the worst for him, in such terrible cold.

Back again, to the place he had been to a short time ago, placing flowers, struggling emotionally. Now it seemed worse, but he was driven on by the need to ensure his family was happy. As much as he struggled emotionally as he walked, he still felt a sense of hope, that with doing what he was about to do, he would find some strength for the future, an answer to all things in all of their lives, because they all depended on each other so much. Finally in that moment it became clear, that he would have to take these steps, that he could trust things would work out, because it just seemed as if it were meant to be.

Slowly, Stan walked up to the place he had left the flowers. They were still there, covered in snow, but clear enough. He looked around, full of hope, just a whirlwind of emotion, waiting for Arthur to come running to him, full of joy, the same kind of whimsy that he knew he should have seen from him the moment he entered their home.

Arthur wasn't there. Stan was alone in a place he knew he should accept, and determined that he would try harder, do better, accept the love of his mother's dog. It would still be difficult, but for all of them he would try, because they were all worth it, and so had she been.

There was little point in waiting around longer. The clock from the nearby St Elphin's Church rang, signifying it was eleven o'clock at night, that time was moving fast, Christmas Day fast approaching. He would have to go and finally confront that which he had ignored for too long.

The roads as he drove no longer seemed to matter. It wasn't too far in a car, but he could only imagine how it must have been for Arthur. His mind wandered again to that day, when he had found her, how Arthur must have felt, running out as he did. It was understandable in that moment that he might not focus then and there on the needs of a dog, but afterwards, having shunned the thoughts of the past, he knew he should have done better for him.

Finally he arrived at the top of the road. It wound in a semi-circle, into a small row of neat bungalows. Hers had been there, in a place he hadn't visited enough, back when he could. Memories flooded back, forcing him to tears. They were tears he should have shed long ago, and memories he should have acknowledged long before. Now he did, accepting his loss, and ready to accept she was gone, his beloved mother.

She had been such a fine woman, so powerful and strong in his life, such a fighter. She was the compass that gave him direction in life, the benchmark on how to be a good man, and driven him on to be happy, and a good person for his family. All he could think about were what ifs.

The car moved along as if it had a life of its own, towards the house. Of course someone else would have moved in, because life goes on, that was fine. For all that, it didn't make any of it easier. Stan parked away from the house, in a small parking area which was too dark to make out. He switched the car off, with it the lights, and sat a moment. Taking a deep breath, wiping tears from his eyes, he opened the door and stepped out.

Stan looked on, over at the place he had visited for so long, finally accepting there was no perfect way to live life, just that you had to be there, and you had to care, and he did.

Each step was slow, not just because of the snow and ice, but because of the emotional resistance he had. A voice nagged at the back of his mind, but it only became clear to him what it was as he finally stepped up to the front garden, and looked at the door. That door, when he had opened it and stepped through and seen her, and allowed Arthur to run out, it seemed as if mentally it were opening again to him, and in his mind, in his imagination he was stepping through, but not doing anything differently, only now he was able to accept that, that he had done the same as anyone else would. It was alright.

The voice nagging at him was his own conscience, telling him he would be fine, it was all fine. It wasn't his voice he could hear, but his mother's, full of love, telling him to be happy.

A small metal gate sat open, before the darkened doorway, no lights inside. Stan stopped, looking at the house, at the pathway leading up to the door. Arthur sat looking back at him, each looking at one another, silently.

Stan kneeled down, ignoring the cold and wet, taking in a deep breath.

"You finally found your way home then, Arthur?" he asked, struggling to speak as tears rolled down his cheeks.

Arthur wagged his tail, as he was wont to do, standing up and slowly approaching Stan. He walked along the path, at first wary, emotionally uncertain himself. For him the perfect ending would be that she would open the door and laugh, and ask where he had been. They both knew it would never happen again, but for Arthur, seeing Stan there, as he held his arms out, he knew he had a new home to go to, others who would care for him just as much. Arthur met Stan's arms as he wrapped them around him. He nestled his head in Stan's chest, closing his eyes, feeling the warmth and emotion, and all the love that he would be given.

Both accepted the way things were, and how they were always going to be.

"Come on, boy," Stan said, standing up slowly. "Let's go home."

Arthur wagged his tail again, looking up expectantly. Together they walked off, back to the car.

CHAPTER SEVENTEEN

"Billy."

"He's well asleep."

"He is. I guess say it a bit louder."

"Billy," the voice came again, a little louder.

Finally he stirred. Pulling the covers away from his face a little, he looked out, trying to see. It had been a difficult night full of tears and thinking about what had happened and might be.

"Mum," Billy asked instinctively. He tried to sit up a bit, remembering it was Christmas Day, time for presents and for the celebrations to begin. Then another memory came to him, last night, Arthur. He wanted to ask, but couldn't give life to the words, for fear he would hear the worst, that he would begin to cry and never be able to stop.

"Merry Christmas, Billy," Abigail said. She was stood in the doorway to his bedroom, with Nancy behind her. Both were smiling at him. Then Billy looked again, to see his father stood with them. They were all looking at him, but he couldn't tell what they were thinking. Was it understanding, were they going to rush and comfort him? It was still Christmas Day, and even if the worst had happened, they could still go and find him.

Everyone paused for a moment, looking at Billy as he looked at them. Finally he couldn't take it anymore, bursting out with it. "Did you find him? What happened, Dad?" he asked, struggling to say it.

Stan nudged Abigail aside, moving slightly to the front. "Take a look under your bed, Billy," he said, smiling at him.

Billy pushed his covers off quickly, before slowly leaning over, peering under his bed. A tail wagged. Two gleaming eyes looked at him, a dog under his bed, looking him straight in the eyes.

"Arthur," Billy shouted, tumbling upside down off his bed. As he did Arthur crawled quickly out, instantly making a fuss of him, licking his face, tail wagging once again so much his whole body shook. Billy wrapped his arms around Arthur, as Stan, Nancy and Abigail all joined in, sitting on the floor, hugging each other.

"Welcome, Arthur, welcome to your new forever home," Stan said, at which they all agreed.

It was the best Christmas present any of them could ask for. Arthur was where he belonged, in a home full of love, knowing he would have a family of his own, always.

The 'Happy' End.

Did you enjoy this book?

If you did, please consider leaving a review on the Amazon website. Good reviews encourage writers to write as well as helping to promote our creative works to others. Whether it is a few words or a few sentences, if you could spend a few moments of your time with this, it would be much appreciated.
Thank you.

ABOUT THE AUTHOR

DJ Cowdall is the author of the hugely popular 'The Dog Under The Bed Series'. He is a British author, having spent many years writing and publishing short stories, now writing novels of all types.

Released January 2018, his novel 'The Dog Under The Bed', is a charming and funny tale about a stray dog in need of a home, which has received a huge response from readers.

He has also authored a book about his time living in Africa and his experiences with his two amazing dogs, titled 'Two Dogs In Africa'.

Following the success and acclaim of 'The Dog Under The Bed', DJ has released a follow up titled 'The Dog Under The Bed 2: Arthur On The Streets', which is available now on Amazon worldwide in Kindle and paperback.

Also available from DJ Cowdall are a varied selection of books, such as the 'I Was A Teenage Necromancer' series, 'The Kids of Pirate Island', and 'The Magic Christmas Tree'.

He is the father of one daughter, Maya, and she is his biggest fan!

Check out his website at:

http://www.davidcowdall.com

Sign up there for his newsletter and for details on forthcoming novels and events.

Feel free to contact him any time at:

djcowdall@gmx.co.uk
https://twitter.com/djcowdall
https://www.facebook.com/DJCowdall
https://www.goodreads.com/author/show/15502553.D_J_Cowdall

Made in the USA
Monee, IL
14 October 2020